I0577645

BROKEN HERO

BROKEN PEAK PACK
BOOK 1

BY JULES CRISARE

BROKEN PEAK PACK

Broken Hero
Broken Sage
Broken Mage
Broken Rebel
Broken Crown
Broken Witch

HIDDEN RUNAWAYS

Hidden Trouble

BLACK HILLS VENDETTA

Wolf's Retribution
Wolf's Revenge
Wolf's Reckoning (*coming to Kickstarter in 2024*)

BOX SETS

Broken Peak Pack eBook Bundle Volume 1
Broken Peak Pack eBook Bundle Volume 2
Broken Peak Pack Omnibus Collector's Edition (*Kickstarter Exclusive*)

SILVER SENTINEL NOVELS

Destined Heir
The Last Immortal Mystery Files (*coming to Kickstarter in 2023*)

SENTINELS OF THE SILVER ORB

BROKEN HERO

BROKEN PEAK PACK
BOOK 1

BY JULES CRISARE

SILVER ORB BOOKS

BROKEN HERO

Copyright © 2021 by Jules Crisare
First electronic publication: August 2019 as Broken Alpha
First print publication: August 2019 as Broken Alpha

All Rights Are Reserved. No part of this book may be used or reproduced in any manner whatsoever without written permission, except in the case of brief quotations embodied in critical articles and reviews. The unauthorized reproduction or distribution of this copyrighted work is illegal. No part of this book may be scanned, uploaded or distributed via the Internet or any other means, electronic or print, without the author's permission.

This book is a work of fiction. The names, characters, places, and incidents are creations of the author's imagination or have been used fictitiously. Any resemblance to persons, living or dead, actual events, locale or organizations is coincidental.

The entirety of this book is created by a human without the assistance of AI. A human wrote this book. A human formatted the ebook and designed the interior layout of the print versions with legally licensed fonts. And a human designed the cover with legally licensed images. *Designed by J. Crisare*

1222pbk

ISBN: 978-1-948603-35-5 (pbk.)

For those who travel along the less traveled roads. There are more of us out there than you might think, and we'll gladly share what we know about the path ahead.

PROLOGUE

A History of Shifters & the Role of the McCallisters
—from Edna McCallister's journal

SINCE the beginning, the Great Shifters took flight and ruled the skies. From their lofted place they oversaw the lesser shifters, such as the wolves, bears, and coyotes. The Great Shifters left the humans to their belief the lesser shifters kept them safe from the razor sharp talons of the Griffins and the fiery breaths of the Dragons.

In actuality, the Great Shifters never bothered with the mundane lives of the humans. Man posed no risk to the Great Shifters and remained outside their concern.

It was the witches, wizards, and vampires who caused the Great Shifters concern. If any one group became more powerful than the others, a massive war would upend the delicate balance between the supernaturals, Great and lesser Shifters, and humans. For that reason, the Great Shifters watched the supernaturals and interfered to keep any one faction from gaining more power than the others.

But the Great Shifters knew a war was coming and accepted their fate. However, they prepared for the future. The strongest of the Great Shifters, a griffin shifter, found a human mate and hid her away from the lesser shifters and supernaturals. The Great Shifter lived with his mate as a man and started a family. In time she gave him children, none shifters themselves, but all carried a griffin inside them.

When the war came, the Great Shifter bid a last farewell to his mate, but left her his wealth, home, and a secret.

No one could know what slumbered inside his children or his children's children. The blood of a Great Shifter was strong and would be passed down, never diluted, through the generations. When the time was right, and Great Shifters were needed, the griffin would wake and the Hero would be born.

CHAPTER ONE

GPS pinged their location as somewhere in the center of Appalachia. The file, open on the tablet in Vixen's lap, sent them to the isolated region of the eastern mountain range. It made sense on paper, or in this case, on screen. That was before she had examined their target's details.

The target was headed towards a region they knew to be a refuge. A sanctuary of sorts. The military couldn't send a team into the area without causing problems. Instead, they would send in a special unit to eliminate the target.

Men and women who fought private wars, either for their government or the highest bidder, didn't run to their families. They ran away. They separated from parents and siblings. The calls from family inviting them to the holidays went ignored until the calls stopped coming. If that didn't work, they died. Or at least invented a death. But those were complicated and messier than convincing your family you didn't care about them.

There was no way their target was headed to the heart of his family. Especially not if he thought he was in danger. He'd lead that danger far away. Running home wasn't the only clue the details weren't kosher. The little voice in Vixen's head posed questions that Vixen couldn't answer.

Despite the signs in the file pointing to the rural and isolated area of West Virginia far away from any of the major highways, Vixen couldn't shake the feeling that something was off. The voice in the back of her mind had yet to fail her, and she didn't plan on ignoring it now.

Turning to the passengers in the back seat, she leveled her gaze on the man sitting behind the driver. He refused to look her in the eye. Normally she didn't mind men not looking her in the eye. After all, she spent years cultivating a reputation as a bringer of death. But that was with her enemies, not the men and women she routinely pulled out of shit situations after the government exhausted all other resources.

"You're sure about this intel?" Vixen waited for the member of the special forces team assigned to work with her to meet her gaze. It never happened.

"It's good." The answer came from the driver. He had been the only one willing to say more than a few words to her since she climbed into the armored SUV in Virginia.

She could ask for more. They wouldn't question her want for further confirmation, but the little voice, the guardian angel who lived inside of her head, spoke up.

They won't give you what you want. Use your time better.

Either the men in the SUV didn't have the answers she wanted or they wouldn't give them to her. Vixen lifted her chin in an approximation of the nod so many men in the military used as a way of greeting or acknowledgment and returned to studying the file on the tablet.

The data was off. Sure, it had a name and a picture, but never, in her sixteen years of service, had they given her a target that was perfect. All the cues were there—isolation, distrust, paranoia, damage to his family, growing resentment, and disappointment in not finding help. And finally, the death of his sister. That was what bothered her. The profile was a textbook version of an individual whose intent was to wage a one-man war against the government and country she swore to defend at all costs. Even at the loss of her humanity.

The streets turned to roads and the heavy truck bounced along the pot-holed ridden surface. Rows of well-maintained, if old, houses devolved into what could only be described as shacks. She tracked the scenery through her peripheral vision. Not in appreciation of the beauty of the landscape, but to keep track of her surroundings.

Why the fake target?

Vixen didn't need to look far for an answer. It was the same answer to why they placed the target in such an isolated location and insisted a team accompany her. The time had come for her retirement. She didn't think a military team would have agreed to it, though. The military was loyal to Vixen. At least those who didn't consider her a legend or myth. If the men with her weren't military, then they were mercenaries.

Mercs couldn't be trusted. They sold themselves to the highest bidder and didn't question the ethics of the assignment. Vixen might not be the most moral of women, she had enough red in her books to guarantee a one-way trip to hell, but she had ethics. She couldn't say the same for her mercenaries in the SUV with her.

The GPS declared the estimated arrival time to be less than thirty minutes away. Assuming Vixen could trust the GPS. Thirty minutes of studying maps that hopefully hadn't been manufactured with the rest of the file.

Not an ideal situation, but she had found herself in worse places. Besides, even if someone doctored the maps, they would probably be accurate enough to be an asset instead of a hindrance. It wasn't what the maps told her, but what they didn't tell her.

The maps, clock, and GPS became her focus. After five minutes it was obvious the details had been shifted. Not in any significant way, so someone would notice with a cursory looking over. Whoever tweaked the GPS just moved the image or screen to be five minutes ahead of reality. Either the one tasked with the job was lazy, or possibly knew the real target and wanted to help Vixen. By using the GPS image, she reconciled the maps with her mental maps of her current location and their destination.

Once they stopped, she wouldn't have much time. A minute or two tops before they realized her stalking off to survey the entry point was her exit strategy. An exit that didn't include a bullet through the back of her head and an anonymous grave. For the first time since Vixen gave up her humanity, nerves struck the center of her chest like a boot from an enemy combatant.

Complacency will kill you every time. You know that. You aren't complacent.

The voice in Vixen's head returned her to the present. She brushed away the nerves with a quick shake of her head.

War.

It wasn't just the name of the town they drove through. It was the state Vixen was about to enter.

She needed to be ready for it.

CHAPTER TWO

THE young males of the pack were fighting. Again. They fought all the Damn time now.

As they reached maturity, their wolves urged them to find their rank within the pack. And as the young males of the pack matured, the need for a pair leading them became a necessity.

Bray pressed his face against the palm of his hand and bit back the curses threatening to break free.

A healthy pack had two Alphas. A male and a female. Usually mates. He didn't need anyone to tell him he needed to find a female. The ache his wolf caused him was enough of a wake-up call that the time for Bray to take a mate had long passed. But not just any female would be able to handle the young male wolves that made up his pack.

Dominant wolves with issues were a concern for any pack, but when an Alpha took on several of those wolves, the problems compounded.

Bray was doing his best to wrangle a pack of misfits, but he failed as often as he succeeded in keeping them in line.

The woods at the edge of the front yard of the lodge called to his wolf. Recently, the woods called to him more and more. Instead of spending time with his wolves, the way a good pack Alpha did, Bray spent his time patrolling the Broken Peak Pack's territory alone. The isolation was the only thing that satisfied his wolf and kept him from leaving to hunt down a mate.

Someday, hopefully years from now instead of months, one of the idiots in his care would challenge Bray, and he'd lose the pack. Until then, Bray would do what he could to keep his wolf calm and give his band of misfits a stable environment before they left to establish their own packs.

He stared at the forest. Less than a hundred feet away from the front of the lodge. The urge to run tonight was stronger than ever. But instead of patrolling the borders, his wolf wanted to head to the waterfall.

Thirty seconds. That was the time left before she could make her move, and the mercenaries emerged from the SUV with their equipment. The guns they would use to take out their target.

Vixen's arms hung down, and she gave her eyesight a few precious seconds to adjust to the darkness of the night. No visible tension. No hint she was going to run.

The sounds of the forest mixed with the sounds of the men working behind her. She did her best to ignore the ambient noises, unless the rustling leaves came from the men making a faulty step. Those were the sounds she needed to keep track of.

Fifteen seconds. Adrenaline pumped through her body in anticipation. Fight or flight. Every human and animal knew it well. The brain's attempt to prompt the body into surviving at all costs.

The problem, at least for Vixen, was that she didn't run. Ever. She always fought. And she always won. If she didn't, she wouldn't be alive and running for the first time since being recruited. Running went against her training, but the voice in her mind had explained fighting wouldn't end well.

Three men, all of whom were likely trained for this mission, lowered her chances of survival. Vixen could eliminate one threat, probably even two, but three well-trained men, intent on completing their mission, decreased the probability of Vixen being the last one standing. Instead, she would be the first one running.

Five seconds. Her feet pressed against the soft dirt as she avoided the fallen branches. At least it was springtime and most of the noises coming from her passage through the forest couldn't be easily discerned from the rustlings, hoots, and chirps belonging to the denizens of the woods.

The shouts coming from behind announced the discovery of her absence. The swearing confirmed her suspicion she was their target.

Veer right.

No path to the right. More opportunity for noise, but also more opportunity to hide. Vixen didn't know the terrain. She'd either have to outrun her pursuers or out-maneuver them. Neither prospect was favorable. Keeping her breath even and her eyes on the ground in front of her, Vixen wove through the woods, charging further into the unknown. The unknown was better than the known. The known meant death.

Through the soft huffs of her even breaths, Vixen's ears picked up a sound in the distance. Water. Running water slapping against rocks.

"Got her!" One of the mercs shouted.

Vixen couldn't tell which of the three men picked up her location, but the man qualified for a stupidity award. Announcing your presence to the target was top on the list of things not to do when hunting someone. Especially when it announced your location.

She lengthened her stride. The river would camouflage her location and offer a place to hide.

The pop of the sound barrier breaking from the speed of a projectile leaving the muzzle of a gun didn't give Vixen enough time to evade the bullet. It did, however, give her time to prepare for the burning and accompanying crippling pain as the hot metal bored into her right thigh.

Don't stop.

If Vixen hadn't been shot in the leg and wasn't still being chased by men who wanted her dead, she would have stopped to argue with the voice. Like she needed any further motivation to keep going. She dug her feet into the ground, covering more of the terrain as she increased her speed. Heat radiated from where the bullet lodged closer to her hip on its path from the entry point at her thigh.

Seconds remained before the adrenaline left her body and the burning turned to a hurt that would knock her off her feet and give the men the perfect opportunity to execute her. Euphemisms like retirement, elimination, or cleaning up could be used, but they wouldn't change the result.

Her booted feet splashed into the river, and she ran along the shoreline. Entering the water would just slow her down. She needed more time. More distance between her and the gunman.

Another pop, but the aim was off and the bullet missed her. Boots pounded against the ground from her left. If the team was smart, the second member would come from the right while the third steered her in the desired direction. She just needed a break in the river. A place where the current calmed and she could hide in the dark, still water.

Get in the river. Now.

Logic and reason said stay on the shore. The voice disagreed. Long ago Vixen decided the voice was her brain responding to her surroundings and analyzing the input at a faster rate than her conscious. She listened to the voice and waded into the middle of the river, fighting both the slippery rocks and the current as they struggled to take her down. Maybe her voice was on to something. Drowning. Death at her own hand was better than death at the hand of another.

Before she thought more about the end of her life, the current swept her feet out from under her and the water pushed her towards the roaring sound she hadn't paid enough attention to because of the bullet wound. She pulled her feet back under her and charged through the water. The resistance wore down her strength faster than the wound in her leg or the loss of the adrenaline so necessary for her survival.

Vixen reached the edge of the river before it dropped over the ragged edge of the land and bounced against the rocks to pool thirty feet below. If blood hadn't been seeping down her leg and the adrenaline hadn't been retreating, Vixen would have dove over the side and taken her chances with the depth of the water below. In fact, she was about to plunge over the edge when a third pop pulled her attention away from the waterfall and back to the real problem.

Her distraction likely saved her. Instinct turned her body to the right as she fought against the urge to look behind her. The bullet cut through her shoulder instead of her back and into her lungs. The force of the second bullet entering her body combined with the limited balance from the first bullet and sent her over the waterfall. Instead of a controlled fall, she tumbled down, banging against the rocks and branches until by some miracle, she dropped into deep enough water to stop her body from being broken even more than it was.

The water from the falls pounded on her, holding her below the surface and stopping her from finding the oxygen her body desperately needed to survive. With her eyes open, staring into the darkness of the bubbling water surrounding her, Vixen's consciousness floated away as the current yanked her limp body further down the river.

Three gunshots echoed through the woods. They came from the waterfall.

Guns going off in their woods were common, but these shots hadn't come from guns used by most of the residents. Someone was trespassing. Someone who didn't know the tradition of asking permission before hunting on another's land, especially land owned by Bray.

Bray pressed his fingers to his lips and let loose a shrill whistle. The high-pitched noise hurt his own ears, but it stopped the fighting.

The youngest, Tevin, rubbed his hand over an ear, but still didn't release his grip on Jackson, the oldest and strongest of the young males. "Damn it, Bray, why'd you go and do that for?"

Bray exhaled and ignored Tevin's question. "Jackson, take Leighton and Finley. Head north and check that Roose and Mac aren't over-sampling their own shine again. Tevin and Allard, you two sweep to the south."

Tevin and Allard grumbled, but did as ordered. Leighton and Finley walked to the edge of the woods, but stopped when Jackson didn't immediately follow.

Jackson stared back at Bray before dropping his gaze and lifting his chin in a recalcitrant act of submission.

"What are you waiting for, Jackson?"

"The shots came from the east, Bray."

Bray offered Jackson a curt nod. "Yeah, they did."

"So why are we going north and south instead of east?"

"*I'm* going east."

Jackson looked over his shoulder at the other two young men waiting for him before returning his gaze to Bray. "Alone?"

"Check on Mac. He's too old to be out in the woods alone, and if he heard the shots, he'll be wanting to investigate." Bray ignored the question and added just enough strength behind his words to force compliance from Jackson. Bray learned early on that if he answered any of the young men's questions, he'd spend a good hour answering more questions. They were worse than three-year-olds asking why.

Jackson joined his packmates, but dragged his feet the entire way.

Bray strode to the east, unbuttoning his shirt and jeans as he walked. At the edge of the woods, he stripped off his clothes, leaving them in a messy pile by the trunk of a tree. He glanced up at the sky, specifically at the moon, and uttered a silent prayer to the silver orb. The moon wasn't yet full, so he'd have to use his own power to shift. Not that it made much of a difference, except he needed to concentrate more when he released the wolf from his body.

No magic, no flash of light, no loud noise, and no sparkling lights accompanied the shift. The transition was instantaneous, and when complete, a large black wolf stood in the place where Bray once stood.

He lifted his head and scented the air. On two feet, his senses were better than a human's, but in wolf form, his senses were even better. It wasn't hard to determine the intruders' general location, and he headed toward it.

Whoever invaded his land upset the animal side of his nature, and Bray wasn't inclined to hold it back. Not at the fast lope his wolf wanted, but at a quick trot. The urge to run towards the danger and destroy the trespassers surprised Bray. His dominance came to a forefront during his youth, manifesting in unpredictable behavior and uncontrollable urges to test the strength of others in his pack. It wasn't until Bray left his pack and he moved to the valleys of the Appalachians that his need to fight settled to a manageable level. Since making the Appalachians his home over twenty years ago, his wolf refused to acquiesce to Bray's influence.

The stink of three men assaulted Bray's nose, and he slowed to a silent walk. Adrenaline, sweat, and gun oil. It wasn't a usual combination. Another scent lingered in the air. Blood. But it didn't belong to an animal. Or a human. Bray scented the not-human blood, but it came from the opposite direction of the men. He paused in the woods, looking between the sources of the two smells. His wolf wanted the men, but wanted to find the source of the blood more.

"You sure she's dead?" A man's voice carried through the forest and the wolf's ears perked. He turned his head towards the sound and pressed his ears forward.

"She fell over the falls and I didn't see her surface. Waited five minutes. I don't think breathing underwater is one of her skills. And she went over as soon as my shot hit. She twisted, at the last minute, but my bullet hit its mark." A second voice answered.

"Let's just get out of here. If we're caught, we can't blame them for her death." A third voice, this one was softer than the others. Probably further away.

So close. He could stalk the men easily since they hadn't bothered to keep quiet. They wouldn't know he was there until he took one of them out, and by then he'd have faded back into the woods. But the wolf's instinct stamped on the man's instinct. Every part of his body urged him to the source of the blood. Bray wanted to destroy the trespassers, but his wolf needed to find the not-human female more and refused to surrender to Bray's will. Before Bray decided to turn away from the men, car doors slammed closed in the distance and an engine revved.

Without the men's presence tugging at Bray's senses, the wolf focused on finding the female. The trespassers might be gone, but there was still someone else in the woods who didn't belong, and he needed to find her. The blood scent was simple to follow, but following its path would waste time. The men revealed where Bray needed to start his search. At the bottom of the falls.

Unless someone knew the woods well, they would have to travel at least a mile in either direction before finding a safe point to descend and then travel another mile back to the base of the waterfall. But Bray knew the woods better than anyone else in the area and his four paws eased the steep descent.

By the time Bray made it to the base of the falls, the scent was so faded, he couldn't pick it up along the shore. Either she was under the water and dead or further downstream. A soft whine threaded its way from his throat, and he clawed at the loose soil at the river's edge. Everything pointed to the not-human female being dead, but he wouldn't return home until he found her.

The current was strong. Even if she was dead, and he hoped she wasn't, the river would have carried her away from the falls. As he moved along the shore, he used his nose to search out scents that didn't belong in the woods and his eyes to discern movement. He finally spotted something in the water almost half a mile downriver and charged after it.

The woman clung to a rock that poked above the surface of the water, or maybe the river threw her body against it. Either way, her head was above water.

The wolf couldn't drag her to shore, but the man could carry her. Bray focused on pulling the wolf back into his body. Before the transition completed in entirety, he reached for the woman. Cradling her body in his arms, he scooped her out of the river. From what the men had said, he expected to find blood covering her head and face, but everything above her neck appeared intact.

The shallow rise and fall of her chest reassured the anxiety swelling up from the center of his gut. An anxiety he didn't understand, but he knew it came from his wolf. Bray picked up his pace. Running through the woods on two feet wasn't ideal, and being naked made the journey worse. Even though his wolf was large by anyone's standards and could carry a human, or not-human as the case may be, without a problem, he couldn't carry an unconscious female.

The stench of blood assaulted his nostrils and her body slid in his arms. The reminder of the woman's injury pushed him to move faster. It would be a risk to bring someone outside of the pack to their home, but he couldn't examine her in the open and he certainly couldn't treat her in the middle of the woods.

A sharp gasp of breath from her lips drew his attention, and he glanced at her face. The powerful lines of her jaw under the bruised flesh, the full lips beneath the split skin, and the straight nose behind the old blood. Her dark blond hair strayed from the tight braid. Despite her marred face, the female was striking. Not beautiful in the conventional sense, but she would turn the head of every male in any room she entered. Bray couldn't see her eyes behind the closed lids, but he noticed a small scar ran through the center of her left eyebrow.

Bray shifted her weight in his arms, holding her closer. Her body might be lean, but it was still dense. She was heavier than he expected. Her waterlogged clothing could have caused it, but Bray thought it was more likely her body was more muscular than the females he was used to. The wolf not only heightened his senses but increased his strength as well, so her weight made no difference. It merely added to the mystery of who she was and why someone, three someones actually, had shot her.

By the time he broke through the clearing to the house he built into the side of the mountain, the woman's blood coated his arms and dripped down his legs.

"Don't give up. We're almost there." Bray huffed out the reassurance intended for both of them.

CHAPTER THREE

AN old man, wiry and stooped over from age, stood in Bray's open doorway. "Well, bring her in. I have your bedroom set up."

Bray ignored Mac's presence as he jogged up the stairs of his front porch and into the house. He could thank the old man later. He'd also ask how Mac knew he was needed. Mac had brought all the lamps into the bedroom along with the dining table. A sheet covered the table, but Bray didn't know if it was to protect the table or the woman.

As soon as he set her body on the hard surface, he stepped back and took a breath. The first deep breath since he found her body in the river.

Mac tossed Bray some clothes. "Get dressed. You don't want her waking up and you standing there with your dick waving in the wind."

"They shot her." Bray pulled on an old pair of jeans and a worn flannel, but buttoned neither.

"I know." Mac worked a pair of scissors through the woman's clothes, stripping the ruined garments from her with a methodical efficiency despite his arthritic fingers. "I heard the shots."

"Did you see the boys?" Bray found the small table holding the tools to treat the wounds and brought it closer. The less he had to move after he examined her wounds, the better.

"Yes, but I doubt they saw me." Mac stepped back from the now naked woman and lifted his head.

Bray met his stare, seeing the same things as Mac. Scars decorated the woman's body. Old bullet wounds mixed with knife wounds. The worst marks followed a pattern that might have been the result of torture. "Who is she?"

"I know you don't believe, Bray, and you don't have to. But you trust me, and I'm telling you she's important enough for you to shelter her."

"That doesn't answer my question, old man." Bray clenched his hands at his side.

"She's important to us. That's all you need to know. And right now, she's not safe anywhere else."

Bray took a deep breath and looked at the injured female. "How long does she need to stay?"

"As long as it takes," Mac answered. "But we have to make sure she stays alive first."

Vixen's shoulder burned, almost as bad as the fire building in her hip. Death wasn't supposed to come with aches and pains. Not that she believed anything came after death. Ignoring the philosophical debate about the end of life versus the afterlife, she took an inventory of her situation.

She was on her stomach, lying on a hard surface. Even with her eyes closed, light pushed through her eyelids. She could hear men talking, but her brain wasn't parsing out the words or able to put them into any discernible order. The pain of her body stunted her brain's functioning. She took a breath through her nose and the scent of iron combined with wet dog hit her. There was another familiar smell, but she couldn't place it. If someone sat her down and forced her to, she would say man, but testosterone didn't have a smell that she knew about.

Vixen focused on the sounds surrounding her. Three distinct voices belonging to men. No sound of a woman. At least not in the same room with her. Assuming she was in a room.

Someone poked at her shoulder, and her body rebelled against the pain. What the hell were they digging around inside her shoulder for, and why were they using a hot poker?

You were shot. Twice.

The voice reminded her of her weakness, but it didn't take away from her real predicament. She didn't know where she was or who she was with. Friend or foe?

Friend.

That insufferable voice was more certain than ever, but Vixen couldn't put her training behind her. No one was a friend. An acquaintance who needed something? She had plenty of those. But Vixen didn't have friends the way others did.

Whoever was in the room with her focused on her injuries. All the better. Vixen clenched her molars together, preparing her body for the pain she was about to inflict on it. Her hand darted to the hand poking at her shoulder and she grabbed the wrist while rolling to her back and off the table. As she swept her body to the floor, she swung her leg at the man poking at her hip. When her foot didn't make contact, she blamed her lack of coordination on not having a mental map of her environment. A man couldn't avoid a kick he never saw coming. The owner of the wrist didn't fare as well.

"Ow! Shit! Brayyyy!" He clutched at her hand as she twisted her wrist and applied more pressure.

Vixen couldn't overpower a man with strength alone. She relied on her knowledge of the body and how nerves worked. The same nerves in her own body shouted their protest at her decision to change from a prone to an upright position.

The man fell to his knees in front of her.

Friend.

She pushed the voice into the background and stared at the man standing in front of her. The one her foot missed when she kicked out. He was tall. Several inches over six feet at least. And muscular. His body looked like it belonged to a young man, one of the special forces teams she worked with, but it contrasted with his weathered face. Dark brown eyes, crinkled at the corners, stared back at her. His gaze shifted between her hip, shoulder, and face. Her gaze never moved from his face.

Bray. That's what the man on his knees in front of her called him. She studied his appearance. He might have had a young man's body, but the smattering of gray streaking through his black hair and the creases in the corners of his eyes belonged to an older man.

Bray held his arms out in front of himself and took a step back. The man on his knees pulled away from Vixen, but she twisted his wrist and pulled his arm up. While he screamed, her own body joined his voice with its own scream of protest, but she ignored it.

"Fuck, Bray, do something!"

"What do you want me to do, Jackson?" Bray's hands spread out, and he pushed his palms to the ground in what Vixen assumed was a calming gesture. He looked from Jackson's face to Vixen's. "Lady, we don't want to hurt you. But you're bleeding and we can't stop the bleeding if you're going to keep Jackson here on his knees and in front of you."

A chuckle, bordering on a cackle, came from the corner, but Vixen didn't shift her gaze from Bray.

"We aren't the ones who hurt you, lass. Let Bray here fix you up, then you can ask all the questions you want." An old man, stooped over with rounded shoulders, shuffled into the middle of the room and into Vixen's line of sight.

Vixen narrowed her eyes at the old man and shifted her gaze between him and Bray. She ignored Jackson, already removing him from the equation. She could take him down if they went after her. Vixen might not survive and make an escape, but at least she'd take one of them out.

Friend.

"Shut up!"

Vixen's shout caused the men to back away from her. Even the one with his arm wrenched up and behind his back. His movement tightened the pinch on his nerves.

"Fuck, it hurts Bray!"

The old man stepped forward, tilting his head to the side curiously as he studied Vixen. "Who are you talking to, lass?"

It had to be the pain. She'd been through worse, but never because of a blatant betrayal. That betrayal had to explain the voice's volume and clarity. Before it was a mere hint, a clue pointing her in the direction she needed to go. It was easy to think of it as being her unconscious. Her brain sharing what it knew without Vixen actively having to parse through her experiences. Now, the voice had grown louder, became a presence, almost a resident. Something she couldn't explain away.

"Who are you?" Avoid the question by asking another question. A tactic well-known and used by most three-year-olds, but it didn't make it a terrible option.

"I'm Mac, and you already heard about Bray and Jackson." The old man stepped closer. "Who did you tell to shut up, lass? Me?"

Vixen took in the basic room. The log walls and wooden floor were relatively clean. Several lamps added to the light hanging from the ceiling. They must have brought in more lights. Everything about the room screamed its primary use wasn't a hospital room. And the lack of security implied it wasn't a holding facility either.

Something tickled at her palm wrapped around the man's wrist. She ignored the distraction, not willing to risk breaking her line of sight to the other two. Bray's stare lowered and so did Mac's. Vixen was no longer the focus of their attention. The man whose wrist she held was.

"Lass." Mac took another step towards Vixen. "Why don't you let go of Jackson and then let Bray here finish what he started. We'll give you clothes and you can go on your way or you can stay and ask your questions. We won't keep you here against your will. But if you stay, I think you might find the answers to some of your questions."

Mac spoke as though he read Vixen's thoughts. It should have frightened her, but there was a soothing manner to the tone of his voice. Like he was speaking to a wounded animal.

Friends. Listen.

The voice was loud enough to distract Vixen from the present situation. Something she would never have allowed to happen before she discovered her impending retirement. She released the man and stepped clear of him. The distance wouldn't be enough to keep her entirely safe, but it would buy her valuable time if he turned on her.

"Jackson. Go." The command in Bray's voice rolled across the room.

Jackson scrambled from the room and didn't look back. From the way he responded to Bray's order, Bray was the leader of whatever group she had fallen in with. If Jackson had been under Vixen's command, she would have corrected the potentially fatal mistake of not checking his six.

Mac shuffled to the table and pulled off the sheet. He tossed it to Vixen, who caught it with her good arm and held it in front of her body. Not that she cared about her nudity, but the sheet was more than a cover, it became a barrier. No matter how weak, it satisfied her primal need for protection.

"Sit down, lass. We need to stitch those holes in you closed to stop the bleeding." Mac stepped away from her and held his arm out to the table.

When Bray kept his distance, Vixen took one step to the table. "I can do it myself."

"You can reach the hole in your shoulder? And there's still the bullet in your hip. The bullet's not in a great spot and we need to get it out." Bray didn't move, but he watched her tentative progress across the floor.

"Where did the other one go?" Vixen tightened her grip on the sheet and pressed it closer to her chest.

"Jackson? He wasn't going to be much help, so I sent him away." Bray took one step closer. He raised his eyebrows and lifted his chin towards the small table holding the limited selection of medical tools. "May I continue?"

Vixen reached around her chest and over her shoulder with her good arm. Her fingers poked around at the flesh. The location made stitching the wound herself problematic. She nodded once.

Friends.

Vixen growled at the voice in her head, and Bray's eyes widened. He looked over at Mac while tilting his head to the side toward Vixen. She watched the exchange, curious as to the silent communication that she recognized as being something usually established after teams worked together for years. She couldn't decipher the meaning, and her eyes narrowed in frustration when Mac shrugged.

"You know our names, lass. What's yours?" Mac leaned against the wall and looked around Bray's shoulder at her.

Her name? An innocent question under most circumstances, but this wasn't most circumstances. However, no harm would come from telling them. It wasn't like anyone in the room would understand its meaning. "Vixen."

Mac's face split with a wide grin, still visible beneath the thick beard on his face. A beard that looked as though it had never been shaved once he started growing it. "Like a fox?"

"I suppose." She didn't understand the humor he found in her name, but some of the tension left her body when he didn't recognize it for anything other than a term used to describe a female fox.

Bray took another step towards her and she watched his approach, but didn't pull away. Every muscle in her body told her she should run. But the voice stopped being just a voice once she sat on the table and prevented her from bolting. Stupid voice.

Stupid girl.

Vixen was starting to hate the voice in her head. Even if it had saved her life.

"Lie down, I want to work on getting that bullet out of your hip first." Bray picked up a pair of tweezers or pliers that resembled a medieval torture device, but didn't look at her.

Once more her body behaved in a way she didn't fully control, and she found herself stretched out on her stomach across the table. "Leave the one in my shoulder. It will work its way out. Eventually."

"Planning on it." Bray pressed on the sides of her wound where the bullet had entered her body on her upper thigh. "Where'd you learn to take a man twice your size down like that?"

He referred to Jackson, the man who left. Vixen couldn't tell if he was impressed with her or disappointed in his man. "Training."

Bray chuckled. So did Mac.

The old man offered his opinion. "Jackson's gonna be sore. You watch your back around him."

Who said Vixen was staying around long enough to need to watch her back? Bray poked at the wound and Vixen flinched.

"Sorry. I don't have anything for the pain." Bray spoke with a softness that soothed her. Well, soothed the voice inside her mind.

Vixen's eyes fluttered closed, and she tried to fight against the urge to sleep. An urge she couldn't explain and closely resembled the lack of control that came with drugs. But she hadn't taken any drugs.

Silly girl. Friends. Will help you. Now sleep.

If sleep didn't weigh so heavily on her, she would have been more concerned about the presence living in her mind. A presence that hadn't made itself fully known until she neared the isolated region of the Appalachians that was supposed to be her grave site.

CHAPTER FOUR

BRAY crossed his arms over his chest and stared at the closed door. The woman, Vixen, thankfully fell asleep while he poked around. He extracted the bullet and closed the wounds without her waking once. She was currently sound asleep on the table. Neither Mac nor Bray wanted to move her and risk the chance of her waking and doing her impression of a superhero on them.

"What aren't you saying, Mac?"

"She took Jackson to his knees and barely broke a sweat. And she did it while injured." Mac leaned against the wall next to the door and stared at the ground. "She's here for a reason, Bray. You might not be ready to believe it, but in your heart you know it's true."

"She's not like us."

Mac snorted. "She's not human either. No way she takes Jackson down as fast as she did if she was just human."

"She's crazy too."

"Why do you say that?" Mac looked up.

"She was talking to someone who wasn't there. Remember? You asked her who she was talking to."

"You ever hear the legends about the half-breeds? Human in all appearances, except they're faster and stronger? Maybe something pushes them towards survival? Something they don't understand." Mac shoved his gnarled hands into the pockets of his grungy overalls. "They say an animal lives inside them, but it can't come out."

"She's not a latent. I've seen plenty of latents and everyone can sense the animal inside them. She doesn't have a wolf or anything else inside her."

"Didn't say she was a latent." Mac shrugged. "From what the legends say, it's more than the human and animal sharing the same space. Instead, they've blended together."

"You're the crazy one now, old man."

"But just think for a minute. You got all the rejec-"

"Don't. They aren't rejects." Bray corrected.

"Fine, are misfits better? They don't fit in packs. Neither did you. You ever stop and wonder why you have enough wolves for a full pack and every one of them is dominant? In the past hundred years, have you ever heard of a pack emerging full of dominant wolves?"

"Sheesh, old man, I don't have time for your riddles and mysteries. I have an injured woman and five overly curious males, lurking down the hallway hoping to hear something I wouldn't tell them otherwise, yet to deal with tonight."

"It's time you took a mate, Bray. You know it, I know it, even the boys know it. But you aren't going to find a good bitch to help you lead this pack of misfits because you don't got nothing to offer her."

"I don't need a mate, Mac. We're doing just fine on our own." They weren't. But Bray didn't want to admit to anyone, not even the young males, that he'd have to make changes or risk the sanctuary turning into a battleground.

"You don't need a mate who's a wolf shifter, Bray, but you saw how she handled Jackson. Now, the way I see it, you can either close the door on it and ignore the gift for what it is. Or you can do what you can to figure out why a female who isn't a wolf, but sure as hell ain't human either, landed on your front doorstep."

Bray pinched the bridge of his nose between his thumb and forefinger. "We've all heard the stories. But they're just that, Mac, stories. Some fairy tale the older generation shares with the pups to explain how we came to be. It's a myth, nothing more."

"What if it's not a myth? What if shifters are an evolutionary step away from the kind like her? The not-humans." Mac mused about the legends. "Part of the problem is our isolation. There's no way to keep track of the stories or trace those stories back to the source."

"Says the man who's lived alone for his entire adult life."

"Well, yeah, because my kind are loners. But we have those same legends, except most of us don't believe they're just legends. Hell, I bet you could talk to Roose and Gareth, both loners too, and they'd have the same stories."

"Mac, you and Roose and Gareth aren't wolves. Just because coyotes and bears and cats believe in a half-breed myth doesn't make the stories any more true."

"All legends grew from a grain of truth." Mac grinned and nodded to the closed door. "Maybe this grain is bigger than you thought possible."

Bray was slowly losing patience with the round about conversation. "Just get to the point, old man."

"Packs need an Alpha pair to remain healthy. You don't have an Alpha pair and your boys are getting old enough and strong enough to poke at what their wolves see as a sickness. If she can take down Jackson, she can handle your boys." Mac tilted his head and studied the closed door. "You could do worse than her as your mate. Have you stopped to ask yourself why you brought her here?"

"It was closer."

"Don't lie, Bray."

"Shit, Mac, she's not a *wolf*." He combed his fingers through his hair and banged the back of his head against the wall. "And no one deserves a life with these idiots. But she's not one of us. You and I both know an Alpha can't take a mate that isn't like them. It's a death sentence for both."

Mac pushed off the wall and turned his back to Bray. "Keep telling yourself lies and you might just believe them one of these days. That female landed at your doorstep for a reason, Bray. She took down Jackson while wounded and in a lot of pain. She also trusted you enough to fall asleep while you fixed her up. I'm not sure what more the moon needs to show you before you're willing to believe."

Bray watched the old man shuffle out. He should have sent one of the boys back home with Mac to make sure he arrived in one piece, but Bray was pissed at the old man. Mostly because Mac didn't say anything incorrect, but it didn't mean what he said was right.

Mac said Vixen needed to stay with the pack to keep safe, but Mac also told her she could leave. Bray had no intention of keeping her prisoner, but he didn't want to wake her just to tell her she could leave if she wanted. The female needed sleep.

She might not know it, but Bray saw the signs of exhaustion, and her wounds didn't help matters. For the time being, he'd push the image of her intelligent green eyes and long blond hair out of his mind. He'd ignore the lean lines of her muscular body. And he'd pretend he never saw the layers of scars covering her skin.

Vixen was a fighter. Mac might be right that she was strong enough to keep the boys in line. But she wasn't his kind. Bray couldn't afford to think about her as anything more than a guest.

Bray turned and headed deeper into the lodge. The half of the house built into the mountain that sated the wolves' needs for a den. The sound of the boys bickering greeted him before he stepped into the kitchen. He stopped in the doorway and leaned against the wall. The boys quieted down at his arrival.

"Who is she, Alpha?" Tevin asked from his place at the stove where he stirred the stew they would eat for their late dinner.

Bray grinned at Jackson, wondering if he shared with his packmates that the woman had taken him down. "No idea. But she's hurt, and she was on our land when it happened. We'll offer her shelter and food until she's strong enough to move on."

"Where's Mac?" Jackson straightened on the stool where he sat and tried to look over Bray's shoulder.

"He went home." Bray sighed and pushed off the wall. "Allard, make a bowl for our guest and bring it to her along with some water. More broth, less meat. We don't want her to get sick."

The young shifter hopped to his feet and hurried to obey his Alpha. At least one of his merry band of misfits listened to him.

"I don't think I have to remind you, Allard, but she's not one of us and doesn't know about us." Bray watched Allard hurry out of the kitchen with the food and drink for Vixen then sat down next to Jackson. "You feeling better, Jackson?"

Jackson delivered a curt nod and kept his gaze lowered. "She might not be one of us, Bray, but she's also not one of them."

As cruel as shifters had been to the boys when they had been kicked from their packs, the humans had been worse. Humans didn't understand the normal behaviors of a dominant young wolf, and any shifter kicked from a pack usually found himself in a group home, or worse.

Mac pulled Jackson from one of those homes, and Jackson had never gotten over it. Until Jackson could get over his hate for humans, he'd never be able to lead a healthy pack. Maybe Bray should have sent Jackson with the food for Vixen.

"Mac agrees with you." Bray reached across the counter and grabbed a slab of bread. He picked at the crust while considering his next words. He needed to share Mac's suspicions with the pack. Even if Bray didn't believe the stories to be more than legends to scare shifters away from mating with humans. He only wanted to explain it once, though, so he'd wait until Allard returned from his chore. "We'll discuss it at dinner."

Jackson glared at Bray, but remained silent. Jackson had been overpowered by the female... Even the female shifters who were strong enough to become Alphas would have difficulties overpowering a wolf as strong as Jackson. That was part of the problem facing Bray. He needed a mate, but she had to be strong enough to keep his ragtag pack in line.

When he watched Vixen's strength as she put Jackson to his knees, Bray had a brief glimpse of a possible future where his pack could finally have an Alpha female and he could have a mate.

Not that he wanted the whole fated mate thing like some Alphas from other packs had. But he wouldn't mind a partner. Someone who could help him raise his misfits into strong wolves who would eventually become Alphas in their own right.

Bray didn't have time to linger on his thoughts for long. Allard stomped into the kitchen, and everyone looked up at his noisy entrance.

"You could have warned me she was bat-shit crazy, Bray." Allard rubbed his hand over his already swelling cheek. "She's hot and all, but she's insane."

Bray's lips lifted into a reluctant smile. "What did you do?"

"Probably just stood there." Jackson looked down at the dark red mark on his wrist where Vixen had gripped him with a strength no one expected.

"Nothing. I just dropped off the food like you said to do and she hit me." Allard dropped his hand, and the swollen flesh of his jaw showed the hints of a darkening bruise. "I think she cracked my jaw."

"You'll heal." Bray chuckled and looked down the darkened hallway towards the room Vixen occupied. She took down two of his wolves. Strong wolves. And he knew it wasn't because his boys weren't trained. "Leighton, get some bowls for Tevin. Jackson, I think there's some beer in the fridge."

As the younger wolves moved around the kitchen, gathering the items for their dinner, Bray watched them bump into one another in a good-natured camaraderie with a hint of rivalry. He counted down the seconds until it would turn into a fight for dominance. It was a miracle they still had dishes with the frequency of the fights.

Tevin filled the bowls and placed them on the island counter they would eat on before the ribbing and teasing turned to grumbling curses and the bumping turned to shoving and outright punching.

Bray couldn't tell who was fighting who, but from the smell of things, a few of the boys were close to a shift. Something that couldn't happen. With a resigned breath, Bray stood, pressing his hands down on the counter as he leaned forward. He opened his mouth, but it wasn't his voice that emerged.

"Oi."

Five heads turned towards the kitchen doorway. Their fists frozen in mid-punch and their eyes wide.

"I've had quieter nights sleeping in war zones."

Bray turned and studied the woman standing there. By all rights she shouldn't be out of bed, much less walking around, but she appeared steady on her legs. Legs he couldn't see beneath the sheet she had wrapped around her body and was holding against her chest, but remembered what they had looked like when he stitched her up. Scarred skin hinting at prior wounds covered hard muscles and did nothing to make her legs less attractive.

CHAPTER FIVE

VIXEN'S fingers tightened around the empty bowl in her hand. She learned early on that she never knew when she'd get her next meal and to eat when she had food available. She also had the help of the damnable voice in her head urging her to finish the stew and find more.

Which was why she ventured out and followed the voices to the kitchen. However, nothing prepared her for the steady stare of six men. Most men looked away when she met their gaze, seeing something inside of her that hinted at the danger she could bring, but these men's gazes were unflinching.

"You cut my clothes." Vixen didn't know what else to say, and the loss of words angered her. Only the voice in her head calmed her frayed edges.

Bray, the older man, the one who stitched her up, didn't look away from her, even as he spoke to another. "Finley, there's a trunk in storage with some old clothes that might fit our guest."

The smallest man, which wasn't saying much because all of them dwarfed some of the ops teams she had worked with, looked over his shoulder at her as he hurried out of the kitchen through a door she hadn't noticed.

Her mind was off. She wouldn't miss anything as basic as a second entry point. Maybe she hit her head on a rock during her fall?

No. You're safe.

What? The voice made no sense. Not that holding conversations with a voice living inside her head made any sense either.

Nothing made sense.

Bray stood, and Vixen stepped back. The man had to be six and a half feet tall, and stepping away was better than leaning her head back until she had a crick in her neck.

Laughter echoed in her mind.

Bray lifted his hands and held them up, palms out, while smiling at her. His attempt to come across as a non-threat wasn't working. "We don't have any women's clothes here. You'll have to make do with the boys' clothes."

Vixen nodded. It made sense in a way she wasn't willing to examine too closely for faults. She took a deep breath, taking in a lungful of air through her nose, and the aroma of the stew beckoned her further into the kitchen. Where the smile from the man failed at comforting her, the scent of dinner seduced her. "Thank you."

Bray tilted his head to the side and followed Vixen's progress with warm brown eyes that hinted at curiosity. "Would you like more stew?"

"I was worried someone gave me the wrong bowl," Vixen looked down at the empty bowl and then back up at Bray. "It looks as though this one belongs to Tevin?"

Jackson punched one of the young men's shoulder. "If you write your name on something, it doesn't make it yours."

"Yeah, well, at least I didn't pee on everything while yelling mine." The man, Vixen assumed he was Tevin of the autographing notoriety, snapped back.

Bray chuckled and patted the empty stool next to him. "Join us. I can't vouch for their table manners, but I vow no one will hurt you."

Tevin reached across the island counter for the empty bowl and Vixen stretched to give it to him before stepping to the stool. Once settled so the hard wood didn't press against the wound on her thigh, she re-tucked the sheet. Bray looked down at her feet and lifted an eyebrow.

Vixen tucked her boots under the bottom of the sheet and hung her heels from the bottom rung of the stool. They might have cut off her clothes, but they left her boots intact.

"You are free to leave whenever you want, Vixen. However, if you wish, you are welcome to stay."

Yes. Stay.

Vixen growled at the voice. Tevin dropped the full bowl to the counter. The stew splashed over the edges. She didn't miss the look he gave Bray or the slight nod Bray gave Tevin in return. Bray mopped up the spill with a napkin, but didn't meet her gaze. The others pointedly looked away. She found comfort in their avoidance tactics. It was something she was used to.

"A few hours' rest, some clothes and food, and you won't see me again." Vixen snatched a piece of bread and dunked it into the stew before pushing the too large bite in her mouth. She'd need to load up on carbohydrates if she planned on covering the miles she needed to get clear of the area.

No!

Bray's fingers tightened around his spoon until his knuckles turned white. "You were shot. Twice. You can't heal in a few hours."

Vixen finished chewing the bread and swallowed before speaking. "You said I could go whenever I wanted."

"I don't want to see my skills with a needle and thread go to waste. At least wait until you don't risk tearing the sutures open. Not to mention, you don't know the fallout of that hip wound. The bullet might have gone in at your thigh, but it hit your hip."

If a voice could nod, Vixen's was bobbing its head up and down with enough enthusiasm to give her a headache. She dunked the bread into the stew again and crunched the hard crust between her molars. With a full mouth, there was less chance of the voice taking control and saying something she wasn't prepared for. Since when did a subconscious behave as a separate entity.

Unless she was crazy. But was being certifiable a better option than having a separate identity living in her head?

The only sound in the kitchen was Vixen chewing until the man, Finley, returned with a large trunk. From the ease with which he balanced it on his shoulder, it couldn't have many clothes inside. Then he dropped it and the trunk landed on the rough wooden floor with a loud crash. Vixen flicked her gaze between the trunk and Finley. From the noise it made on impact, he shouldn't have been able to carry it on his shoulder with such little effort.

Don't worry. Eat.

Vixen ignored the voice and her food. "The sooner I leave, the safer you'll be."

Bray set his spoon down with an exaggerated sigh. Apparently, she frustrated him. "The men after you think you're dead. The longer you stay, the safer you'll be."

Vixen stared at the trunk while she considered Bray's words.

"Finley, bring the trunk to my room. Vixen can go through it there." Bray watched her watch Finley as he lifted the trunk with one hand and settled it back on his shoulder.

His reassurance she was safe made little sense. Finley crossed the floor and left the kitchen. Once he left the room, she swiveled her head and stared at Bray.

When things didn't make sense, there was usually someone who could explain the non-sensical. The other men continued their attempts to look anywhere but at Vixen. Except for Bray. He studied Vixen the same way she studied her surroundings.

"How do you know about the men? And how do you know they're certain I'm dead? The last thing I remember was falling off the waterfall, but I also remember the strength of the current. You couldn't have found me close enough to the men to know they think I'm dead."

"Who said I was the one who confirmed the men's belief that you're dead, or that I found you?"

His explanation was logical, but Vixen didn't buy it. His conviction came from first-hand knowledge, and she was sure he was the one who carried her from the river. She covered a good mile at least during her flight from the truck. Another quarter mile down the river after she lost consciousness. While she worked out the logistics from the point, she lost consciousness to waking up inside a house that shouldn't have even been in the territory according to the maps.

She finished her stew. Good food was good food.

Finley stomped back into the kitchen and threw himself onto a stool reminiscent of an adolescent finishing a task forced on him by a parent. "Didn't know where you wanted the trunk. It's by the bed."

His report was for Bray, but Vixen nodded along. Her body made the gesture despite not having a conscious thought to nod. How many other things had her body done without her realizing it?

She bit down on her bottom lip and sopped up the last of her stew with the bread crust. Too many conflicting thoughts barreled through her mind, making it difficult to parse out what she needed to do next. She settled for eating the bread.

Bray cleared his throat, and it sounded similar to a growl. "When you finish, I'll bring you back to your room."

Vixen heard the rest of his words, even if he didn't say them aloud. They would talk then. She could either eat another bowl of stew or she could get some answers.

The decision wasn't difficult. Once she left, she wouldn't get any answers, but she could always forage or steal food.

Vixen finished buttoning the old flannel shirt. It was much too big for her, and she had to fold the sleeves over several times until they hit her wrists and didn't hang beyond her fingertips.

Bray leaned back on his hands on the bed and stretched his feet in front of him. He didn't like the sight of her in the boys' old clothes. He'd prefer her wearing his shirt at least, but if she was swimming in those, his clothes would float off her.

"How did you find me?"

Bray pulled his gaze away from her fingers as they wove the thick strands of her hair into a tight braid, and he looked at her face. He had been wrong. Striking didn't come close to describing her. Vixen was regal and elegant. She wasn't beautiful by a standard measure, but Bray was certain many men had called her that.

Her head tilted to the side, and she raised an eyebrow at him. The gesture was so practiced, but natural. Bray couldn't help himself from smiling.

"If you won't answer my question, I'll grab more food before I head out."

Bray shook his head. Mac was right. She was safer with him than out there alone. Even if she wasn't a wolf, he couldn't let her leave.

Whatever Mac was playing at with his promise to her she could leave, Bray would have to convince her she shouldn't. Considering how fast she took down Jackson, Bray wasn't sure it would be a simple task. "We heard the gunshots and investigated. Then figured out where you'd likely be."

Vixen shook her head. "Try again." She dropped the belt she had been trying to tighten enough to hold up the oversized pants and grabbed a braided rope.

"Why do you say that?"

"Because you're lying." She didn't bother looking up from the ends of the cord as she tied a knot.

"And you're sure of that?"

She glanced up at him and grinned. "Just as sure as I am, the sun will rise tomorrow morning."

"We heard gunshots."

"Well, I would hope so. It wasn't like they used silencers. But how did you know where to find me?"

Damn. Not only was she not-human, but she was also smart. One benefit of young dominant males was they did a lot of stupid things and could be easily convinced of half truths. "I told you, the men who shot at you revealed where they left you."

"But you found me and got me to safety..." From the way she bit down on her bottom lip, Bray gathered she was trying to put the math together so it made sense. It was what he would have done in her place. "Not enough time."

"What do you mean?" Bray knew what she meant, but wouldn't confirm her suspicions.

"I had to be more than a mile from the truck. Even assuming they moved quickly over the terrain, it would have taken them ten minutes to get back if they didn't want to leave anything behind. If you were at the furthest point from hearing them when they left, it would take you..." Vixen moved her fingers along with the calculations her mind was making while looking up at the ceiling. "Seven minutes to reach the falls?"

Bray leaned forward, resting his elbows on his knees. He didn't think she was aware that she gave him a glimpse into the workings of her mind. It was a fascinating show, and he didn't want to interrupt it.

"So seven minutes to where I fell. Assuming you know the quickest way down, but it wouldn't be a direct path, at least not an obvious one. Let's say twenty minutes, give or take from the time they drove off. But ..."

"But?" Bray grinned.

Vixen leveled her stare at him and narrowed her eyes. "Assuming where you found me was minutes away from here, you still had to carry me. And you couldn't have traveled that distance in a few minutes. Ergo, the time I am theorizing it would take you to find me and bring me back here doesn't match with reality. *How* did you find me?"

"Something told me where to look and I didn't have to search for a path. There's a hidden trail. It's difficult, but it's not impossible." Bray sympathized with her plight. Plus, he was concerned she'd focus on the details of her time line until she realized it would be an impossible task for a man and not just improbable.

"Something?" Vixen stepped closer toward him, balancing on the balls of her feet, as though she was ready to pounce on him as quickly as she had pounced on his words. "What kind of something?"

"Let's call it instinct."

"Instinct is just your brain computing experiences, determining the different outcomes based on those experiences, and giving you a nudge toward the response that is likely to lead to the best outcome." She took another step, or bounce since her heels never touched the ground, closer. "Do you regularly find bodies in the river?"

It was too bad Vixen wasn't a wolf. She'd make a wonderful mate to him and an Alpha to the boys. "No, but I've hunted enough."

Vixen brushed away his answer with a wave of her hand. "Nope. Not buying it."

"Why don't you believe me?"

"Why won't you answer my question?" She took another one of her bouncing steps towards him.

"I did. You just didn't like my answer." Bray watched her approach. She moved in a way that wasn't deliberate. Or at least she didn't appear to be aware that she was moving closer to him instead of keeping her distance.

"I didn't believe your answer." She stopped just out of his arm's reach. Maybe she was aware of the distance separating them, after all.

"Who were you telling to shut up when we were sewing you up?"

"No one." Vixen answered too quickly, but she didn't look away from him.

"Why were you so certain I lied?" Bray was curious. He knew she wasn't human, well not-human, but did she?

Vixen lifted a shoulder, "I just was."

"Did something tell you I was lying?"

She narrowed her eyes at him before schooling her expression.

"Well, something told me where to find you." At least she wouldn't hear a lie. Or whatever made her not-human wouldn't hear a lie and then tattle on him.

Vixen looked over at the closed door. "Someone's outside."

"Five young males, to be exact. They think they're being secretive." Bray didn't plan on losing whatever trust he gained by lying about knowing the peanut gallery was eavesdropping. "They're curious."

"Curiosity killed the cat."

"Well…" Bray wanted to laugh. There wasn't a less appropriate idiom. "While I don't doubt that you could probably kill them, I don't think you would."

She shrugged and offered him a small smile. Instead of answering him, she slowly turned, taking an inventory of the bedroom. They hadn't moved the table back to the kitchen and there wasn't much else in the room, at least nothing identifying. Bray didn't have a need for personal items besides his clothing, and none of his clothing was unique from what the others wore. She completed her circle and rested her hands on her hips.

"Who are you, Bray?"

"I asked that same question about you earlier, when I was sewing your skin back together."

"I wondered how long it would take you to stop being polite and ask the question."

"Who are you? I told you, I already asked that question." Bray wasn't sure where she was headed, but the wolf perked up during the conversation. Something he normally didn't do. Conversations bored his wolf.

"That's too obvious of a question to ask." Vixen smiled, as though she was enjoying the conversation as much as Bray's wolf. "Did I underestimate you?"

"Your badges from battle aren't my business." Bray answered.

"But they are. If I am here, they are very much your business. Especially the two fresh scars."

"Is that why you want to leave? You think it will keep us safe?" Bray re-evaluated his original assessment of the female. "I told you, they believe you're dead. And no one will talk, if you're worried about that."

"Do you always assume every person shot on your land didn't deserve it?"

"No. But then I rarely find strange females unconscious in a river after being hunted down and shot." The wolf wanted to go to Vixen, but Bray held back. She was like a frightened animal, ready to flee at the slightest move.

Bray might not trust what Mac told him about Vixen, but the old man had never steered him wrong before. If Mac thought she needed to stay in the territory, Bray would have to convince Vixen it was in her best interest not to leave. And that it was her idea.

"How do you know about sewing up wounds and removing bullets?" Vixen's mind jumped topics like a squirrel from tree to tree.

On cue, scuffling broke out from the other side of the door. Bray stood and in a few steps strode across the wooden floor. He yanked the door open into the room and five males looked up from what resembled a violent game of Twister. "A day doesn't go by that one of these idiots doesn't need some kind of medical intervention."

"A good workout would burn that excess energy out of them." Vixen crossed her arms under her chest, but the ghost of a smile remained.

Bray shook his head at the males, still frozen in the tangled knot of limbs. Bray looked back at Vixen. "I tried. It just makes it worse. Though I'm not sure how that's possible."

"They haven't worked out with me." Vixen narrowed her eyes at the males.

All five of the young males disentangled themselves from each other and stood up straight. They weren't stupid males, far from it. They might do stupid things, but if she could take down Jackson and hit Allard, her "workouts" would probably leave them wishing for a swift death.

"You can't work them out if you aren't here." Bray closed the door and leaned against it. He was close enough to touch her, to reach out and hold her. Stupid wolf. Holding the female wasn't an option. At least not at that moment.

For the first time in years, Bray's wolf wasn't pushing him to seek a mate. If Vixen left, he was sure the urge to hunt his mate would return with a vengeance. And this time isolated runs wouldn't satisfy the wolf.

He heard the stories about mates destined for one another if fate allowed for their paths to cross. Not that Bray believed in destiny or fate, but he always figured something special accompanied the recognition of finding the right one. There was nothing. No burst of power. No electric spark announcing the attraction. Instead, he just knew. The same way his wolf knew.

The female standing in front of him was the perfect mate for his pack of misfits. For his wolf. For him. He just needed Vixen to figure out she was destined to be his mate. But before Bray could convince her she was his mate, he had to convince her to stay.

Bray needed to earn her trust.

"Let's go for a walk."

CHAPTER SIX

BRAY led Vixen out to the front porch and settled her onto the swing hanging from the porch roof. He created a nest of pillows for her and wrapped a blanket around her legs while being careful of her hip.

She cleared her throat. When Bray looked up from the meticulous task he set himself with, she lifted an eyebrow at him.

"If you won't call it instinct, then call it a compulsion." He looked away with his admission. "I can't ask you to trust me if I'm not willing to show you trust."

"How does tucking a blanket around my legs relate to trust?" She nodded toward the shadows in the yard formed by the moonlight hitting the trees of the forest. "The peanut gallery slipped out the back."

"You can see them?"

Vixen squinted at the shadows. "No, but you won't stay alive for long if you don't pay attention to your surroundings."

Bray ignored her observation. As though he expected a different answer from her. When she didn't give it, he changed the subject. "Vixen, I want to show you something. But I need you to stay on the porch and not move from the swing."

She opened her mouth to laugh off his request, but no words came out. It wasn't for lack of trying. Her voice stopped working. Panic crept up on her. After everything that had happened during the night, from her involuntary retirement to waking up naked among strangers, this was when panic made its appearance?

Trust him. Friend. Mate.

Instead of shouting out the words shut up, like she wanted to, she yelled them to herself.

Maybe the reason for her retirement was because she failed her last psych assessment.

Stupid girl.

Stupid voice.

"Vixen?"

She jerked at Bray's voice, pulling her out of the argument with herself, and winced as her hip bounced against the swing.

"Do you need more pillows, are you uncomfortable?" Bray's need to make her comfortable frightened her almost as much as the voice living in her mind.

Vixen shook her head and tried to speak again. The words came out with no problems, but she still couldn't stand. "I'm fine..."

"Trust me?"

Not really, but she nodded along with his question.

Bray unbuttoned his flannel and slipped his arms out of the sleeves. He was old enough to be a father, but Bray didn't have an ounce of flab on him. The man was as chiseled as the twenty something hotshots who entered the special forces after months of hard training. The only difference between the trainees and Bray was the silver hair sprinkled across Bray's dark chest hair.

Moonlight shined down on him, reflecting against his tanned skin so it seemed as if he almost glowed. The same light also highlighted the scars on his chest, shoulders, and arms. Similar to hers, except they followed no pattern. Bray's scars fascinated her enough that she missed him toeing off his boots and dropping his jeans.

Oh. Well. Bray was big all over.

She blinked. And when she opened her eyes, a huge black wolf stood in front of her instead of Bray. There was no sleight of hand, no flash of light, and no loud noise to distract her. He was just there, and then he wasn't.

The black wolf lifted his muzzle, going white just under the nose, and scented the air before settling his gaze on Vixen.

Mate.

The voice was as excited as a child on Christmas morning.

Friend. Trust.

"If I didn't have a voice living inside my head, I'd say I was dreaming. Instead, I'm either dead and this is the afterlife or I am crazy." She stared at the wolf. His rich black fur on the rest of his body wasn't marred by white strands, but the tips of his ears and the soft hairs inside his ears had turned white. The wolf shared the same brown eyes as Bray. "Or none of the above…"

The wolf stretched his front leg forward, approaching her with a caution that surprised Vixen. Another step. As the wolf came closer to her, she appreciated just how large the animal was. Vixen stood at just shy of five foot ten inches and she didn't have an oddly short trunk compared to the length of her legs, but she sat nose to nose with the wolf. If the wolf sat, the top of her head would hit his chin. The size of his paws eclipsed her hand, and even her feet weren't a match for them.

Reason and rationality told Vixen she should be frightened and planning an escape from the predator looming in front of her, but the voice disagreed. The same voice Vixen was coming to realize wasn't her unconscious or a sign of her insanity.

After spending more than half her life working for the government, Vixen had seen it all. She'd seen stupidity, she'd seen brilliance, she'd seen secrets, and she'd seen the things kept secret from the secret keepers. That Bray might be the wolf standing in front of her should have surprised her, but it didn't. That she didn't know about the secret shocked her. And if she didn't know about it, then the government didn't know either.

The wolf, or Bray, sat in front of her. Vixen had been right. She had to tilt her head back to see the wolf's nose and eyes. His ears, just as big as the rest of him, pricked forward and his tongue hung out the side of his gaping jaw. A jaw with prominent canines that put the knives Vixen used for wet work to shame.

"Well, I didn't run." Vixen didn't believe it was prudent, given the situation, to admit she couldn't run because of a voice that lived in her head. But even with whatever was happening inside of her, she wouldn't have. For the first time in almost twenty years, Vixen wasn't fighting a compulsion to look over her shoulder and move on.

The wolf huffed. Then, in another blink, Bray stood in the wolf's place.

She narrowed her eyes and stared up at the naked man. "You showed me yours, so now you think I'll show you mine?"

Bray grabbed his jeans and pulled them up over his thick legs. He zipped the fly, but left the button unfastened. "You don't have to show me anything. I trust that if, when, you leave, you won't share our secret. And maybe you can give us, me, some trust back."

Vixen glanced toward their audience lurking in the shadows. "Are they like you?"

Bray nodded, "It's not just my secret, but all of ours."

"They'll be watching for reports of a dead body being found. And when it doesn't show up in the next few months, they'll send someone out to investigate. Your secret is more likely to be revealed if I stay than me sharing it."

"Who are they?" Bray pulled his shirt on and settled next to Vixen. He stretched his legs out in front of him and pushed off the porch to start a gentle swinging. "Or is this one of those, you could tell me, but then you'd have to kill me?"

"I imagine a wolf's neck snaps as easily as a man's." Vixen fell back into the persona she created during her employment. If she kept her distance from people, it made relationships impossible and fading away into the background easier.

"You could try." Except Bray wasn't intimidated. "You don't seem surprised."

"There's not much that surprises me." Vixen shifted her weight off her hip and tilted closer to Bray. Neither acknowledged the change of position. "In the desert there are tales. Animals believed to be extinct in the area, but spotted in unpopulated regions. There were tales of wolves roaming close to farms, but no reports of missing livestock."

Bray shrugged and stretched his arm along the back of the swing. "We aren't isolated to one country."

"How have we not learned about you?"

"We're excellent at hiding in plain sight, and humans are great at ignoring what doesn't make sense." Bray played with the end of her braid, but Vixen didn't pull away. The gentle tugging relaxed her. "Look at you, for example."

"Me?"

Bray chuffed a laugh and tugged at the end of her braid. "Yes, you, Vixen. Without knowing your exact job, I imagine, you excelled at it. Haven't you ever wondered why?"

"No."

"Never?"

"Are you doubting me?" Vixen pulled her hair free from his fingers and draped it over her shoulder.

"Did you doubt me when I explained how we found you?"

Vixen didn't answer with words. She looked away from Bray and the peanut gallery. She hoped they were getting a late night's worth of entertainment.

"We're more alike than we are different, Vixen."

"I've never blinked and ended up covered in fur with a tail and four legs."

"No, but you can tell when someone isn't speaking the truth. And you're stronger and faster than most, right? How do you explain surviving despite three men hunting you and having two bullet wounds?"

"Experience and knowing when to follow my instinct."

"By instinct, do you mean the voice inside your head you yelled at to shut up?" Bray pulled her braid, so it hung down over the back of the swing and resumed playing with the ends. "I don't know what you are, Vixen, but you aren't human. I could tell the moment I scented your blood after they shot you."

Vixen reached into the collar of her shirt and scratched at the edges of the wound on her shoulder.

"I'm betting you heal faster too." Bray pressed his toes down on the porch and stopped the gentle sway of the swing. "I hate this, you know?"

"What's this?" Too many thoughts muddied up her thinking, but at least the voice remained silent.

Bray took a breath and pulled her closer to him. Vixen didn't understand why he didn't think she would take off running, but he behaved as though he had faith in her remaining. Or he had faith in something other than her.

"You shouldn't be learning about this from me. I'm the last one who should tell you this."

Vixen slid away from him and pressed her body into the corner of the swing, keeping her weight off her wounded hip. "Then why are you? Why didn't you let me walk out of her like I planned?"

"Because my wolf wants you to stay." Bray reached for her again, but instead of being satisfied with Vixen sitting next to him, he tucked her onto his lap without any visible effort.

Vixen wasn't a small woman. She didn't fit in most men's laps comfortably. But her body fit together with Bray's. He didn't even grimace as she shifted her weight to accommodate the dull ache in her hip. She didn't bother trying to pull away. What would be the point? The voice, or thing that made her non-human according to Bray, wouldn't let her move more than minor adjustments. The voice might have been silent, but its presence hadn't disappeared.

"Your wolf doesn't understand what me staying would bring down on you and them." She waved her hand in the general direction of the young men still lurking in the shadows. Vixen hadn't heard or seen them, but she knew they were still there. The same way she knew where to find the waterfall when she fled her assassins.

"My wolf and Mac are both certain you're supposed to be here. You not running away when you saw my wolf and that you haven't run away from me, makes me think something inside of you believes you should be here too."

"This is a lot."

"Tell me about it." Bray tucked her head under his chin and let out a slow breath. "I don't believe in fate or destiny, but whatever you are belongs here with my wolf. This pack of misfits would overwhelm another female, but you brought Jackson to his knees while in pain. And you took a swing at Allard and didn't miss. For whatever reason, you fit here with these ragtag lost boys."

"So you're Peter Pan and I'm Wendy? If I remember the story correctly, it didn't turn out particularly happy for either of them."

"Well, the Lost Boys didn't kill each other. With this group, death is a strong possibility."

"So less *Peter Pan* and more *Lord of the Flies?*"

"Yeah, but I doubt they'd ever be organized enough to come up with a chant."

Trust him. Trust mate. Trust me. You're safe.

Hadn't Vixen always trusted the voice? She trusted it when she believed it wasn't something separate from her. And that was also before Bray dumped a lot more crazy into her lap.

But no matter how good Vixen was at what she did, she'd make a mistake, eventually. They'd find her and finish the job. She couldn't drag innocents into her fight.

"I'm not a good person. I've done bad things to bad people, Bray. There's a reason my retirement party didn't come with balloons and cake and ice cream. My existence could destroy this country if it ever became known. I'm an avenging angel. I killed our enemies and hand off the credit to special forces so our country has something to celebrate. And I haven't just killed our enemies. I'm a last resort. If I can't extradite you, then I'll kill you." She looked down at her hands in her lap and picked out the invisible bit of dirt under her thumbnail, "I'm a bad person, Bray. They can't let me live and they'll have no problem taking out anyone close to me."

"Why do you think we live so far away from civilization?"

"I figured all your kind did."

"Most have integrated into human society fairly well. Humans would never guess the private club their neighbor belongs to is a pack or clan that meets once a month in an unpopulated area to shift and let their animals run free."

"All right. I'll bite. Why are you so isolated?"

"Because me and this merry band of misfits have wolves who don't do well being civilized. Our wolves are too strong for the Alphas who lead urban packs. The Alphas from the rural packs already struggle to keep their own dominant wolves in line. They won't bring in a wolf they know will challenge them for Alpha."

"Being socially inept isn't the same as being a sociopath. A well-trained and highly paid sociopath, but a sociopath nonetheless."

"Sociopaths are a human thing. You aren't human."

"And I'm also not like you. I can't turn into an animal."

"That could be because your animal is part of you."

"What does that even mean?"

"I don't know. It's something Mac said." Bray wrapped his arm around her waist and settled her closer to him. "Stay a few days more. Give your body time to heal. And while you're doing that, Mac can answer some questions."

Yes!

Vixen closed her eyes. Of course her voice would want her to stay. If she was honest with herself, she didn't mind the idea of staying either.

Another few nights in a bed with a few warm meals couldn't hurt. And it wasn't as though anyone would figure out she survived for a few days. Except for the analyst who put together the intel for the op. If they had been helping her, they wouldn't say anything.

"A few days. That's all." She promised herself as much as she promised Bray.

CHAPTER SEVEN

"YOU need sleep." Bray stood in a single smooth movement without jostling Vixen.

She'd carried enough people out of dicey situations to know it didn't matter how strong someone was, they needed to adjust for the added weight. Yet Bray hadn't changed his stance. He carried her to the door and supported her with one arm while reaching for the handle with his free hand.

"Whoa."

"You okay?" Bray asked.

"You're strong."

"So are you. But I'm guessing you and your handlers made excuses for it." His grumbled answer might have been a growl with what she now knew.

"I never carried someone without having to compensate for their weight."

Another grumble. Something, and not her voice, told Vixen it didn't come from Bray the man, but the black wolf who lived inside Bray.

"If you're off the grid, how do you get electricity or running water without showing up on state or county records?" She looked at her surroundings, taking the time to study the details. The front door led to a large room with oversized couches and chairs. But no TV. Across from the front door was an archway open to a hallway that would eventually lead to the kitchen. Despite it being the middle of the night, the fixtures hanging from the vaulted ceiling did a good job of keeping the shadows at bay.

"Who said we're off the grid?"

"I didn't see this property on any maps."

"Ah. We're not off the grid. We just lie low and are good at hiding in plain sight. An urban pack in Virginia uses one of their dummy accounts as the owner of the property. As far as West Virginia knows, all the bills are sent to and paid for by the name on the account. No one asks questions. The trick is not doing anything to gain attention."

Bray continued into the hallway and entered the room Vixen had woken up in. The windows to the outside placed it in the front half of the house. From the outside, the house looked as though they built it up against the mountain. It wasn't until someone was inside that they realized it had to be built into the mountain by how far back the house went.

He set her down on the bed, then positioned the pillows so she could sit up against the headboard. The bed faced the window and Vixen bet it was a pleasant view during the day.

"Who's Mac to you?" Vixen asked as Bray sat down at the foot of the bed and removed her boots.

"There's a reason this pack is filled with young dominant males. I was one, except my Alpha didn't kick me from the pack when I became a problem. He called in a favor from Mac, and the old man set me up here. There are others living in the region whose animals don't do well in human society. Between Mac and them, they kept my wolf in line. So when a problem adolescent shows up in the human system, we try to bring him here."

"Is this your way of thanking Mac?" Vixen had a similar relationship with a general. He hadn't taken her in and trained her, but he had kept Vixen protected as much as he could. Until the General had a heart attack and was forced into retirement. In return, Vixen had repaid his protection by doing what she could to keep his men alive when things got bad.

"I guess." He dropped her boots to the floor, setting them toes out with the laces ready to go so she could lace them up quickly.

Vixen looked down at the boots. "You aren't military."

"Finley was. No one knows how it happened, but he slipped through the cracks. Foster care, group homes, until the judge gave him the choice of going to jail or joining the Army. Someone was in the right place at the right time and spotted Finley before he outed us. Finley got transferred to Fort A.P. Hill, then lost in the system. Mac and I drove to Bowling Green and picked him up."

"And the others?"

Bray stretched out on the bed, leaning against the foot board and facing Vixen with his arms crossed behind his neck, pillowing his head. "They all have their own stories. Some worse than others. Tevin is the youngest, but he's been here the longest. His Alpha contacted Mac after Tevin lost both parents. He was the first one, the one who started it all. And since we didn't break him, others found their way here."

"Is Tevin the one who signs his name on everything?"

"Yeah. He wasn't good about sharing. Still isn't."

Vixen didn't want to smile or laugh, but it was hard not to when she imagined a little version of Tevin signing his name on everything. "I bet he's good at washing things, though."

"How'd you guess?"

"Because I doubt he limited himself to just signing plates and bowls, and from the looks of this place, you keep it clean."

"My wolf likes a tidy den. I think it helps with the others too. It doesn't matter if they're a wolf or human, adolescent boys need structure to thrive." Bray brushed his fingers over her ankle and when she didn't pull away, he wrapped his hand around her leg, under the hem of the jeans just above her ankle. "They're a mess, though. All the structure in the world won't keep their dominance in check."

"You seem to manage." While Vixen had been spending her adult life hunting down the men and women her government ordered her to, Bray had been playing dad to boys who weren't even his. "Bray? What would have happened to them if you didn't take them?"

"Worst case, killed. Best case, found an isolated area, far away from civilization, and lived a brief life as their animal slowly took over." Bray squeezed her ankle. "Don't get any ideas, I'm not a good male. I'm a good wolf and Alpha, but I'm not a good male. Whether or not I wanted them, Mac would have dropped them off at my door then stopped by every few days to make sure I hadn't done anything stupid with them."

"I'm not a good woman. I'm a good killer. One of the best, but I'm not a good woman." A satisfied rumble rolled through her chest. She couldn't deny it came from her, but it wasn't an involuntary noise and she hadn't caused it. The voice. It was back.

I never left.

Of course not. She'd have to have a conversation with it at some point. Come to some terms of agreement. If she didn't, Vixen had no doubt it would drive her crazy until she didn't need to worry about staying hidden because she'd want to be discovered just to end the madness.

A heavy weight settled on her chest. It didn't have a tangible source, at least not that Vixen could tell. It was a steady pressure pushing against her. She looked up and caught Bray staring at her. But he wasn't looking at her eyes or her face. Bray's gaze focused on her mouth.

"Are you doing this?" She whispered as she rubbed her palm across her chest, easing the pressure.

"Not me. My wolf. That noise called him. He's pushing against my control."

"Why?"

"He thinks you're his."

Vixen wasn't a stranger to casual sex. In her line of work, relationships just weren't possible, and she wasn't willing to abstain from sex for over sixteen years. She found satisfaction with others in similar situations. Leaders of special forces teams were perfect candidates. They didn't have any expectations and understood she didn't belong to anyone. In fact, after stressful missions, she found the best way to settle the adrenaline was through a night of no-strings sex.

She wasn't planning on staying. A few days at most, then she'd walk away. Vixen had done it before and she'd do it again.

She ducked her chin and closed her eyes. A signal for both Bray and his wolf. Vixen was willing. Would he be?

One moment Bray was leaning against the bed, the next he was on his hands and knees, prowling towards her.

Bray was willing.

He caged her body with his. His fists pushed against the mattress close by her hips and his legs straddled hers.

Bray leaned down until his lips landed on hers. She expected the uncontrolled urgency that accompanied most of her trysts, but Bray was gentle and sweet and soft. He took his time, exploring her mouth with gentle sweeps of his tongue then backing off to using just his lips. When he pulled back and looked down at her, she caught her bottom lip between her teeth.

If the kiss was anything to go by, she'd remember tonight for the rest of her short life. And she didn't want to forget it.

"I don't want to hurt you."

Vixen almost rolled her eyes. "You won't."

"But you're injured."

"I won't break." She nipped at the flesh between his neck and shoulder. Vixen had no idea what came over her. She wasn't a biter and didn't enjoy being a bitee. The one partner who had bitten her, lost a few teeth that night. Biting hadn't been an issue since.

Apparently, Bray enjoyed bites. Which she supposed made sense with the wolf and all.

He hadn't put his shirt back on after their show and tell outside. The cords of his muscles bunched and released as Bray rolled to his back, bringing Vixen with him until she straddled him. It was impossible to ignore his size. She'd seen him naked, but hadn't studied every detail of his body. Perhaps she should have. Vixen dragged her fingers down his chest, along the dips of his defined muscles.

His stomach flexed, and Bray grabbed the blanket, tightly fisting the loose material in his hands.

Vixen met Bray's gaze. "Your eyes... they're almost gold."

"I told you my wolf was close." Bray groaned out the words with a soft growl that sent a satisfied rumble through Vixen. He rubbed his hands along the top of her thighs, careful to avoid her hip while Vixen traced the marks on his skin.

At the moment, they didn't need anything more than light touches, but the reprieve wouldn't last. Something else was driving both of them. The voice said safe, but Vixen thought it was more than that. She couldn't find the right words to explain it all, but whatever was happening, she understood its importance.

Bray sat up, cradling her against his hips as his lips found her jaw and brushed against her skin. He moved his mouth to her ear and whispered, "I know. I feel it too."

In all her life, Vixen had never needed anyone. Or so she told herself. At that moment, with Bray, she needed everything he offered her. Her voice was wrong. Bray didn't just bring safety, he brought peace. Contentment settled over her. For the time being, she was in the right place.

He rolled her onto her back, once more careful of her wounds and his weight. Bray knelt by her side, looking down at her with a reverence Vixen didn't deserve. His hands hesitated above the top button of her shirt. "You'll tell me if I hurt you?"

She nodded. "Yes."

Together they undressed the other. Vixen pulled his jeans down, while Bray stripped the borrowed clothes from her body. Once both were naked, Bray stared down at her. But he wasn't looking at her body. He ran a thick finger over her fresh wounds, already starting the healing process. Even the pain of the bullet wounds had shifted from a sharp hurt to a dull ache.

"You heal fast."

Vixen shook her head. "Faster than some, but nothing out of the ordinary."

"Your bruises are faded…"

"How?" She didn't understand how her body could heal that quickly.

"It's a wolf thing."

"But I'm not…"

"Human."

"Fine, but I'm not a wolf either."

"I told you before, I don't know what you are, but whatever is inside of you, it's healing you." Bray's thumb brushed over the already fading bruises.

Vixen's gaze followed the movement of his thumb. Fluttering sensations landed at the base of her belly. Was it nerves? Anxiety? Vixen couldn't say. She'd never experienced anything like it before.

Bray stretched out beside her on the bed and pressed the palm of his hand between her breasts. Keeping his steady gaze locked on hers, he dragged his hand down her sternum and over the muscles of her stomach before pausing.

"So strong, but so soft."

"So gentle, but so hard." Vixen covered his hand with hers.

Bray's lips followed his hand's path.

Her heart pounded against her chest. Bray lifted her hand from his and placed it against his heart. The slow and steady thump from hers beat in time with Bray's. Her heartbeat matched his.

"What's happening?" Vixen spread her fingers across his chest, stretching until her fingertips reached just beyond the pulsing rhythm.

"I don't know." Pressing a kiss just beneath her belly button, Bray laid his hand over her heart.

"This isn't a wolf thing?"

"No. Well, I don't know. Maybe."

"Maybe?" Vixen squeaked out and Bray chuckled at the noise. His warm breath tickled her skin, and she wriggled away, attempting to evade the sensations.

Bray growled and looked up the length of her body at her. "Woman, you need to stop moving or I am going to lose what little control I have left."

Despite the chastising tone of his voice, his eyes danced with humor and a smile teased at his lips. Bray's gaze slid back down her body, taking in each curve and swell before returning to her eyes. Hunger replaced the humor, and her body warmed under his heated stare.

Vixen swallowed hard, suddenly feeling like a virgin. Whatever she had experienced before didn't matter. It was as though some force had erased her past. Not that it was possible, but a lot of the impossible had become possible in less than a day. If men and wolves could share the same body, why couldn't a woman's past be changed? She laughed at the thought.

"What?" Bray paused from kissing around her belly button.

"Random thought."

"Woman, are you telling me that what's happening right now is boring enough for random thoughts to distract you?"

"No." Vixen reached down and combed her fingers through his hair. She expected it to be coarse, but the dark strands were soft. "I was thinking about the possibility of the impossible."

Bray turned his lips back to her stomach and let out a satisfied grumble. Or growl. Vixen wasn't sure if the wolf or the man made the noise. Her fingers brushed the skin on the back of his neck, teasing him with the similar tickling his lips were doing to her stomach.

Her fingers tightened in his hair. She needed more than light kisses from him. Bray surged up over her body. Even though he braced himself on his elbows, he couldn't support all of his weight with his body pressing against hers. Vixen didn't mind. If anything, she welcomed the reminder she was still alive from the slight discomfort of Bray's hips pushing into her.

Bray's mouth covered hers, planting gentle kisses across her lips. His soft touch distracted her from the slight pressure on her hips and shoulder. "Relax, baby. I'm going to take care of you, don't worry."

Vixen wrapped her arms around his neck and pulled his head back down until his lips once more pressed against hers. She opened her mouth, and he deepened his kiss. Bray ran his hand up the side of her body from her hip to her breast. His thumb brushed once, twice, and a third time over her nipple. Barely touching her. While his thumb worked the sensitive skin of her breast and nipple, his mouth moved lower. Kissing down her neck, along her collarbone, and then down between her breasts before hovering just over her nipple.

He pressed her breast up and lowered his mouth, wrapping his lips around her nipple. The gentle circling of his tongue sent ripples of pleasure through her body and her heart raced.

Bray looked up at her, holding her gaze steady with his as he pressed his teeth into her flesh. Vixen arched, pressing her shoulders back into the bed. She never felt the ache from the added pressure on her wound.

He wrapped his free hand around her neck, holding her steady as he switched his focus to her other nipple and gave it the same attention as the first.

Vixen didn't want him to stop, but Bray pulled away from her nipple with a pop and kissed his way back down to her navel. Only this time, she knew he wouldn't stop at her belly button.

Keeping one hand around her neck, he brought his free hand down her body. His fingers found their destination before his mouth, which was dropping kisses mixed in with nips across her hip bone.

His finger easily slid into her. "You're so wet. Is that for me, baby?"

She couldn't form any words, but she moaned in response. Vixen closed her eyes and parted her legs, inviting more from him.

Bray slid a second, then third finger in, moving them slowly at first before increasing the pace. He played her body, coaxing the pleasure from her then stopping just before she fell over the edge. He kept up the steady rhythm of his fingers. He slid back up her body.

Once again, his mouth covered hers and his kiss swallowed her moans. Her body undulated beneath him, writhing with pleasure. Vixen reached between and wrapped her hand around his thick, hard cock. Together they brought one another to the cusp, but never let the other fall.

"Bray, I can't wait…" She panted out between kisses while tugging him closer to her with each firm stroke.

His chuckle tickled her ear as he nuzzled and nipped at her neck. Opening her thighs for him, she guided him into her as soon as he slipped his fingers out. Keeping most of his weight on his forearms, he rocked into her, inch by inch. Her body stretched around him, accommodating his generous size with ease.

Vixen lifted her hips, speeding up the process, and Bray ground his jaw, barely keeping back a loud growl. Poor man. He wanted to take it slow to keep from hurting her, but she was beyond caring about her injuries. She just wanted all of him. She wanted everything he could give her and more.

When he didn't give in to her body's demands, she grabbed his hips and pulled him fully into her until the base of his cock pressed against her clit, nearly doubling their pleasure.

"You feel so good, baby. So damn tight."

Vixen moaned and squeezed around him as he pulled back slightly before thrusting back into her.

Bray groaned and reached down, placing his hand under her knee to bring her leg up and around him. If it was possible, he went in even deeper as he rocked his hips against hers. His mouth found her nipple again and her fingers tightened into the firm muscles of his ass.

They rocked with each other, finding the easy rhythm of two people comfortable with the knowledge they would both go over the edge of pleasure together. His thrusts grew stronger and deeper.

It was too much. Vixen lost the fragile grip on the control she barely had a hold on. Her body tightened. Her breath quickened. Her head fell back and her eyes closed as the scream of pleasure escaped.

Bray followed right behind her, his body tightening as his release exploded inside of her. He covered her mouth and captured her noises of pleasure.

The waves of pleasure continued rolling from her body until all she was capable of doing was trembling under his weight.

"Fuck." She panted out between gasps for air.

"Fuck." He growled as he slowly pulled out of her and collapsed on his side next to her.

Vixen reached for the sheet, wanting to clean the mess he left behind.

Bray stopped her with a growl. "Leave it."

His body curled around her, one arm going under her head and one leg covering hers. He tucked her against him. It didn't miss her attention that he faced the door and any potential threat. Bray had lied. He was a good man, keeping her safe and protected.

He kissed her forehead. "You need sleep."

Vixen smiled against his chest and nodded her agreement. "Bray?"

"Hm?"

"I'm glad I didn't leave."

"So am I." He whispered back.

CHAPTER EIGHT

A SCREAM yanked Vixen out of sleep.

She sat up in bed, or attempted to, but Bray's arm held her in place against his body. "What's wrong?"

Bray pressed his lips against the back of her neck. "Nothing. Just Leighton. Go back to sleep."

But it wasn't nothing. Vixen knew the sound of that scream well. She had heard it too many times in the past to ignore it now. The sound wasn't from fear, its origin was from pain. Leighton wasn't in pain at the moment, but his mind was reliving the cause and Vixen had to act.

Lifting Bray's arm, she slid from the bed. Grabbing the shirt that had been forgotten on the floor, she pulled it on. The bottom hit just above her knees so she didn't bother with a pair of pants she wouldn't be able to find in the dark. Once buttoned up, she stepped out of the room and padded down the hallway, following the scream.

Vixen didn't have to look behind her to confirm Bray followed. The hallway led deeper into the mountain, sloping downward.

Interesting. Not only was the house built into the rock but also into the ground. Vixen wondered if Bray built the house to double as a shelter in case the government ever found out about them.

The scream led to a closed door and Vixen pushed it open. Leighton crouched in the room's corner, between the bed and a dresser. His eyes were wide open, but he didn't see anything. She stepped into the room, careful not to make any loud sounds, but also careful to make enough noise that her presence wouldn't surprise Leighton when he came to.

She knelt in front of him, but didn't touch him. "Leighton?"

The screaming stopped. His head jerked up at the noise and he blinked. Once. Twice. A third time. "It was a bad dream."

By how quickly he responded, Vixen assumed he used that excuse a lot. And that the others living in the house accepted it.

She held out her hand. "Let's get you back to bed."

Leighton reached out, but hesitated a moment before pressing his palm against hers. She took his weight and pulled him to his feet. No point in giving him a reason to back away from her help, especially since his mind hadn't come back on line from whatever horror he was reliving.

Vixen led him to the bed, and Leighton followed. Once he climbed in, she pulled the blanket up before sitting down next to him. Not knowing for sure what caused the scream, she didn't reach out to comfort Leighton with touch. She needn't have worried. Leighton grabbed her wrist and clung to her.

A soft growl came from the doorway and Vixen looked over her shoulder at Bray hovering in the shadows. She rolled her eyes, but otherwise ignored Bray's outburst and returned her attention back to Leighton.

Neither spoke. Vixen rubbed circles and other shapes on Leighton's back with her free hand and he clutched at her wrist, refusing to let go.

"Nightmare or memory?" She asked.

"Both," he answered.

Vixen didn't need any more information. She understood. "Do you want to talk about it?"

"No."

Again, she understood and didn't ask for more. Whatever caused Leighton's screaming was his story to tell when he wanted to tell it. She wouldn't force it from him sooner than he was ready.

"Right here. Right now. You're safe." She gave him the one thing she could.

She didn't know how much time had passed before Leighton fell asleep. It had to have been quite some time since Bray slunk into the bedroom and sat on the floor with his back against the bed and his body wrapped around her leg. It might have been because of the voice, but she understood. Bray, the man, wasn't holding on to her.

The wolf was.

When Leighton let out a soft snore, Vixen pulled her arm and leg free before standing.

Bray didn't hesitate before scooping her up and cradling her body against his as he carried her back to his bedroom. He didn't let go of her even as he climbed into bed. She didn't struggle against his hold, but hugged him and pressed her body tight against his.

"Thank you," Bray growled.

"For what?" She buried her nose against his chest.

"For Leighton. For my wolf. For everything."

It took a few seconds for Vixen to understand his answer. She supposed she could have gotten huffy and upset when Bray got all clingy, but that wouldn't have helped anyone.

"Thank you, right back," Vixen whispered.

Bray kissed the top of her head. "You need sleep."

Vixen closed her eyes and yawned. Bray wasn't wrong and sleep came quickly.

CHAPTER NINE

BRAY leaned against the open door and watched the sleeping woman who would be his mate, if he and his wolf had any say in the matter. Her chest rose and fell beneath the layers of blankets he covered her with when he woke up and got out of bed. She slept through two fights, breakfast, and another fight where Bray had to push all five males out the front door. Even when Jackson and Tevin rolled into the wall, Vixen didn't do more than exhale a quiet snore.

Either he exhausted her, which filled his chest with male pride, or she hadn't had a good night's sleep in a long time, which filled him with another type of male pride. Regardless of the reason, his wolf released a satisfied growl.

When Leighton's screams came in the middle of the night and Vixen had gone to him, Bray's wolf wasn't happy that she sat in Leighton's bed. Though, once Bray sat with them, giving his wolf the opportunity to recognize she wasn't doing more than comforting a pup, it was all he could do to stop his wolf from claiming her as his mate right then.

If and when Bray claimed Vixen, she'd be bound to him, physically unable to be apart for any significant distance or time. Vixen insisted she needed to leave. As much as Bray wanted her to stay, he didn't want a mating to be the reason. He'd seen it happen and heard the stories. Those matings never ended well. Leighton came from one of them. His mother gave up and died after he was born, leaving her son to be raised by the man who forced the mating. Leighton hadn't told Bray everything, but Bray wouldn't have wished Leighton's childhood on his worst enemy.

No. Bray needed to keep his wolf on a tight leash. The wolf wouldn't be happy, but an unhappy wolf was better than an unhappy Vixen.

Bray returned to the kitchen. His wolf needed to feed the female. He figured bringing her breakfast in bed was neutral in the scheme of things. Once she ate, bathed, and dressed, they would visit Mac.

The old man knew more than he admitted last night, and between Bray and Vixen, he figured they could intimidate Mac enough for him to reveal whatever he was hiding. And then he'd feed Vixen again because it would make his wolf happy. And maybe he'd send the boys out on some task so he and Vixen had the afternoon together. Alone. Without Bray having to break up a fight.

He filled a tray with sliced fruit, bacon, sausage, scrambled eggs, biscuits, butter, jam, honey, juice, both apple and orange, and anything else he found in the fridge that looked edible. To top it all off, he added a large mug of hot chocolate and a cup of coffee. He expected Vixen would prefer coffee over hot chocolate, but his wolf was adamant about the hot chocolate.

Bray stopped his wolf from picking wildflowers to stick in a vase for her. Vixen didn't seem like the flower kind of girl. No, she was a knife and gun kind of girl. He'd have to look through his weapon collection and see if he had one that would be perfect for her. He carried her breakfast into the bedroom and paused once more at the doorway. If going to see Mac wasn't so important, Bray would have been content spending the morning watching Vixen sleep.

She stretched out on the bed, taking up almost all the space. A vast difference from the night before when she clung to him in her sleep, curling up against him and burrowing into that hot space between his body and the mattress.

Shit. Bray needed to convince Vixen to stay. And not just because his wolf demanded it.

The shouts from the young males in the yard carried into his bedroom. He should have sent them into the woods so they wouldn't disturb her. A loud crash followed by an even louder curse came from the yard. Vixen groaned in the bed and pulled a pillow over her head. As though that would smother the noise.

Bray chuckled. Vixen threw the pillow at him, not even bothering to open her eyes. Her aim was true though, and Bray dodged to the side to avoid the pillow hitting him square in the face.

"I brought you breakfast."

Vixen released a little human growl. Bray shouldn't have found it as adorable as he did. Even his wolf raised an eyebrow at Bray's sentimentality. Her nose crinkled as she sniffed the air, and Bray found that adorable too.

But Vixen wasn't an adorable sort of woman. She was strong, resilient, and sexy as hell, but, he reminded himself, not adorable. If she ever learned he called her adorable in his mind, he might find himself with several new bruises or a broken arm.

"Bacon?"

"Among other things," Bray stepped into the room. "I wasn't sure what you liked."

"What sorts of other things?" She sat up in bed and held the sheet to her chest while stretching forward to see what else was on the tray.

Bray sat down on the side of the bed and placed the tray between them. Vixen didn't bother with silverware. She scooped up some scrambled eggs with her fingers and popped it into her mouth. Bray's wolf pushed against him, wanting to witness his mate eating the food he provided. Not that Bray hunted or gathered the food himself. He visited Costco.

Once a month, Bray took one of the packmates and drove to Harrisonburg, where they bought enough food to last anyone else a year. He learned to give the managers a head's up since they bought out most of the meat department and emptied the store's supply of produce and dairy.

Vixen pushed the plate closer to him. "You don't want any?"

"This is your breakfast. I already ate." Both Bray and his wolf bristled at the thought he ate before Vixen. That last bit didn't settle his wolf at all, but they both understood sleep was more important than food.

She shrugged, but continued eating and drinking. After she ate most of the food on the tray, Vixen sat back with the mug of cocoa. Bray's wolf puffed out his chest and preened.

"Thank you for breakfast." Vixen cocked her head in a wolf-like manner and studied him.

Bray nodded to the closed door across from them. "There's a bathroom. It doesn't have a bathtub, but there's a bathtub in the utility room off the kitchen." He said the word bath so many times it stopped making sense as a word.

"A shower's fine."

"I think we should go see Mac right after." He danced around the subject of her leaving.

Vixen lifted the tray and leaned down over the side of the bed to set it on the floor. "We can do that."

Bray watched the breakfast tray's progress. When he looked back up at Vixen, she had let the sheet fall from her chest to pool around her waist. His wolf did an impression of the howling wolf from the 1940s cartoon. He pulled his gaze away from her breasts and forced himself to look into her eyes. "Woman, what are you doing?"

"Well, since I'll probably be leaving at the end of the day, we should take advantage of the time we have together. Right?"

Her logic made complete sense. But he was so taken with her, she could have uttered total gibberish and made the same amount of sense. Bray didn't need to hear the words again. He tugged down the sheet, baring the rest of her body to his more than appreciative gaze.

Bray knelt over her and pulled off his clothes. There was no finesse or seduction in his movements, just an unadulterated need for her. The entire time, he kept his gaze on her. Not once breaking his stare. Bray reminded his wolf that he couldn't claim Vixen. Not yet, at least. Vixen watched him undress, her eyes holding the same appreciation he had shown. Her breath caught as he pulled his jeans free and knelt over her. He laced his fingers through hers and stretched her arms over her head.

A few seconds later, and their bodies came together. Arms and legs tangled together as he kissed her. One more day wouldn't be enough. The bed creaked under their combined weight as they rocked against each other. She fit against him as though she was meant to be there.

His hand collared her throat. Vixen's pulse raced beneath his palm and he savored the sensation, not sure when he would get another opportunity to feel it. "Say you're mine."

Her bright green eyes flashed gold. If he hadn't been looking right at them, he wouldn't have believed it.

Vixen snapped her teeth at the air in front of him, but didn't pull free from his grip.

"Say it, baby. I need to hear it. My wolf needs it."

They stared at one another, neither backing down. She swallowed hard. Once. Then twice. "I'm yours."

Bray slid his hand up her arm and while holding her hands together above her head, he thrust into her. Hard. She lifted up, arching her back to meet him.

He wanted her on her hands and knees. He wanted to take her from behind, slamming into her so she would never forget she was his. But he wouldn't be able to stop his wolf from claiming her. As it was, he already danced along a very narrow line, forcing Vixen to tell him who she belonged to.

Bray bent over her and whispered in her ear, "hold on, baby, this is going to be hard and fast."

She lifted her ass off the bed and he bottomed out, going deeper than before. He drove his cock harder and faster with each thrust. There was no way he would last much longer, but he needed her to come with him. Bray released her hand and reached between them, rubbing his thumb against her clit while her pussy pulsed around his cock.

He sucked and bit at her neck. So tempted to bite down on her tender flesh and leave the permanent mark that would forever tie her to him. Before his wolf took over and branded her neck with his mark, Vixen lost control and screamed her pleasure as the orgasm rocked through her body. Bray followed, deliberately lifting his mouth away from her skin as he exploded inside of her.

Bray collapsed on the bed, careful to keep his weight off her as he pulled her into his arms. "You okay?"

Vixen nodded.

Bray kissed the marks on her neck and traced them with the tip of his tongue. As satisfying as it was seeing his marks on her skin, he let his wolf get too close to the surface. He needed to be more careful.

"Hungry?"

Vixen laughed at his question and turned in his arms so she faced him. "I just had a full breakfast. But shower, clothes, then visit with Mac. Right?"

He'd rather spend the rest of the morning in bed with her, but she had a point. Bray brushed his lips against hers, trailing light kisses over her mouth and nose. They could stay in bed for a few more minutes at least. That was, they could until the shouting from outside got louder and a body slammed into the exterior wall with a thud.

Bray groaned and rolled out of bed. He grabbed his jeans and pulled them on, zipping them up but not bothering to fasten the button. "I should check on the boys before they break through a wall."

Vixen stretched out, and it was all Bray could do not to climb on top of her. Another loud crash, this one was closer to the window. While Bray wasn't worried about someone going through a wall, the window was another matter. He replaced more panes of glass than he cared to admit.

She peered over the foot of the bed and out the window. Perhaps she expected to glimpse the fight that had been going on since she had distracted him with her magnificent breasts. Vixen laughed and pulled the sheet up. "Go. I'll jump in the shower and meet you outside."

Another crash, this one louder than the previous two.

Bray dropped a kiss on her forehead and hurried out to the yard.

Four wolves brawled against one another. Jaws snapped, claws scratched, and blood flowed. Only Leighton remained human. He leaned against the porch, watching the fight.

"You didn't think to stop it?" Bray growled at Leighton.

"I tried." Leighton shrugged.

Somehow, Bray didn't buy that Leighton tried too hard. He figured it was easier to let them tire one another out than stop the fight. But he couldn't have them going through another window. Bray growled low in his throat and headed into the brawl. Using some well-timed kicks and a few punches, he pushed the fighting wolves away from the wall.

"Is she staying?" Leighton asked over the snarling wolves.

"I don't know." Bray didn't want to talk about it with Leighton. He didn't want to talk about it with any of his pack. Besides it being none of their business, at least not until she agreed to a mating and became their Alpha, what did a bunch of twenty-year-olds know about the feelings Bray was experiencing? He crossed his arms over his chest and glared down at the wolves. He'd have to stand between the house and fight, or they'd make their way back to the porch and close to the windows again.

"Have you asked her?"

"It's not as easy as that." Bray didn't want to be having this conversation.

"Yes, it is." Leighton spoke quietly, but Bray had no problem hearing his words. "I hope she does."

Yeah. Bray hoped she did, too. He didn't think it would be as easy as asking her, though.

A wolf, he couldn't tell who, yelped as a set of jaws clamped down on him.

It was going to be one of those days. Bray just knew it.

CHAPTER TEN

VIXEN tugged at the loose fitting clothing hanging from her body. Everything was five sizes too big, the opposite of what she usually wore. However, she couldn't deny the comfort of the worn jeans and flannel shirt, thin from one too many washings.

With a sigh, she bent over and laced her boots up around her ankles, then rolled the jeans down over the top of the boots. Regardless of when she left, she'd need to find better fitting clothing. And hair elastics. She couldn't even pull her hair back. Although, cutting it short might be a better option in the long run.

She combed her fingers through her damp hair and made a mental note to send Bray to town with a shopping list. The less she was seen in public, at least for a few months, the better.

She wished she still had her weapons on her. Bray hadn't given hers back. Her gun and knife must have fallen out during her tumble over the waterfall. Another thing to add to her list. Vixen headed outside, following the noise of the fighting that hadn't lessened so much as it had moved away from the house.

Bray and Leighton leaned against the porch railing. She hadn't realized the porch wrapped around most of the house, at least the part of the house that wasn't built into the mountain.

"I take it they do this often?" Vixen approached the two men.

Bray shrugged, "often enough. I assume blood doesn't bother you?"

Vixen shook her head. Not much bothered her, but she didn't think Bray needed the details. She rested her forearms on the railing and bumped her good shoulder against Leighton's. "You good?"

Leighton jerked his chin in an approximation of a nod. Good enough.

"How's your shoulder?" Bray asked.

"Better. Kind of surprised."

"Save it for Mac." Bray released a shrill whistle, and the fighting stopped. "Change. Now."

Even Vixen felt the weight of the command that rolled from Bray. It was a different heaviness from what she felt with him in bed, but still familiar.

When she had watched Bray change from man to wolf, then back to man, it had been quick and the change hadn't appeared to cause him any discomfort. The same couldn't be said for the wolves in the yard. Their transformation was slow. And loud. Bones and muscles snapped and popped as they reshaped themselves. Several minutes later four naked men lay panting on the ground, groaning in discomfort. All of them had wounds from the fight, gouges from claws and punctures from fangs. But the blood wasn't the cause of their pain.

"I'm heading to Mac's for a bit. Jackson and Tevin, you two clean the kitchen."

"Why us?" Tevin whined.

"Because I don't doubt you started it. I might not know what you two did, but you know, and that's enough." Bray growled out and Tevin had enough sense to avert his gaze while lifting his jaw and exposing his neck. "The rest of you, split up and patrol the borders. I don't expect we'll have visitors, but keep your eyes open for anything unusual."

If Bray was sending a few of the men out, it was an opportunity to find her weapons. Vixen cleared her throat.

Bray looked over at her and raised a questioning eyebrow.

"Any chance of one of them looking for my knife? I must have lost it in the river."

"Leighton, start at the top of the falls, but chances are it went over with her. Check at least a mile from the base."

He looked at Bray and nodded his understanding. Without a glance back at the others, Leighton trotted off towards the woods.

"Well, what are you waiting for? An engraved invitation. Get going."

The other four gathered their clothes and pulled them on as they hurried to follow Bray's commands.

"They're like brothers." Vixen mused at the bickering.

"Brothers don't normally kill each other."

Her eyes widened. Kill? What little of the fight she saw didn't resemble a mortal battle.

Bray chuckled at her response and tilted her head in the opposite direction Leighton headed. "You good enough to walk?"

"I think. Yeah." She rolled her shoulder and shifted her weight from foot to foot, testing her hip. "I don't remember ever healing this fast."

"I have suspicions, but I think Mac will explain it better than I can." Bray wrapped his hands around her waist and lifted her over the railing. He held on a moment too long, before dropping his hands from her waist and picking up her hand. He tugged her along with him.

They walked together in silence. She had a lot of questions, but Bray wouldn't answer her. He deflected that responsibility to the old man she barely remembered meeting. She rubbed a fist over her sternum. The heaviness from Bray's earlier command hadn't lifted.

Bray's grip tightened around her hand, and he pulled her behind him. Whatever he heard put him on the defense. She didn't particularly enjoy that he needed to step in front of her. The gesture rubbed against everything she understood about herself. But she wasn't an idiot and didn't fight his need to protect her.

"Roose." Bray wrapped his arm around Vixen's waist and pulled her against his back.

She peeked around his shoulder at the sound of heavy footsteps approaching. An enormous man, one who made Bray look average sized, stepped out into the clearing in front of them. Paul Bunyan had come to life. Except he had long blond hair and a thick beard covering the lower part of his face.

The giant ducked his chin and scowled at Bray with his arms crossed over his chest. His biceps were as thick as her waist and his legs gave the massive tree trunks surrounding them an inferiority complex. "This the guest Mac mentioned?"

Bray pulled her tighter against his back, only this time she didn't mind. The giant, Roose, could have snapped her in two without breaking a sweat.

"What'd he tell you?" Bray asked.

Vixen couldn't help herself. She had never seen a man as big as Roose and leaned further around Bray's arm. She lost her balance and almost went over, but Bray's arm kept her from falling on her face.

"Enough. Come on. I just brewed coffee. And not the pansy-assed way you and the boys do. This is a real pot of coffee." Roose's beard parted as his lips stretched out in a wide grin, and the deep booming rumble of his voice shook the leaves in the trees.

Vixen didn't blame them for shaking. She would have shook too if Bray hadn't been holding her. Assuming Roose was one of Bray's friends, he was in on Bray's secret or had a secret of his own, and Vixen would have laid down money that Roose's secret wasn't a wolf.

Bray pulled her around, but kept his arm wrapped around her waist. "Roose, this is Vixen."

"Vixen?" Roose pulled his eyebrows together and nearly bent in half to peer at her. He sniffed around her before standing back up. "No fur. I figured Mac got into his shine, but maybe he was right. Come on then, we should have a talk. And we should also probably send Gareth over to check if your house is still standing."

The laughter escaped before she could stop it. Whoever this man was, he knew the boys of Bray's pack. Roose gave her a slow wink and his grin broadened into a smile. Bray growled and pulled her close against him. The smile slipped from Roose's lips, but he gave Bray an understanding nod before turning and heading into the woods. Bray kept his arm tight around Vixen's waist as they followed the giant man's footsteps.

Roose led the way to a small cabin with smoke coming from the chimney. It was a smaller version of Bray's house, except not built into a mountain. Roose stomped his way up the porch steps and into the house, leaving the door open for Bray and Vixen to follow.

Bray guided her to the couch and settled her next to him while Roose opened and closed cabinets in the kitchen. She looked around. The cabin had a single large room with smaller rooms shooting off the back wall. One was the kitchen and the other she assumed was the bedroom since she didn't see a bed anywhere. Similar to Bray's house, she didn't notice a TV, but Roose had electricity and running water from the sound of the tap turning on in the kitchen.

The giant man came back into the main room, holding an old-fashioned coffee pot and three tin mugs, painted to resemble stoneware. He set the cups down and filled them with coffee, then sat in the chair next to the couch. Vixen figured his furniture had to have been reinforced to not even creak when his weight settled onto it.

"What do you think and what do you know?" Roose asked.

"I don't think anything, but what I know is she's here for a reason." Bray counted off the reasons on his fingers. "She heals fast. She took down Jackson, while injured. And she got one over on Allard."

Roose's bushy eyebrows shot up his forehead and got lost in his shaggy hair. "She doesn't smell like fur, but she isn't human."

"Mac mentioned the old legends..." Bray trailed off and looked over at Vixen, as though he wasn't sure she was ready to hear the rest.

For her part, she turned her head from side to side, listening to the conversation that centered on her despite not taking part. She hated this passive crap, but Vixen was nearing forty years old. She had years of learning that sometimes staying quiet rewarded her with more information than if she interjected herself into the conversation.

Except Roose turned his attention to her and learning by listening was no longer an option. His bright blue eyes, so light they were almost silver, bore into her and Vixen rubbed her knuckles against her sternum. Whatever heavy thing Bray had going on, it didn't come close to what Roose could do.

She needed to learn their trick.

Dominant.

Vixen jumped up and yelped. The stupid voice. It had been quiet for long enough that she hadn't thought about it.

Roose's head cocked to the side.

"Oh, yeah, and she has a voice. Or, at least, she calls it a voice." Bray interpreted her outburst.

Bear.

Well, that explained Roose's size, but she didn't need a voice giving a running commentary. "Oh, shut up." Vixen realized how crazy she sounded, growling out the words to no one in particular.

Roose graced her with another one of his beaming smiles. "Her growl is human."

Bray wrapped his arm around her shoulder and tucked her against his side. "But she's not."

"Not animal either." Roose leaned back in his chair and rested his cup of coffee on his stomach. "You know about latents, right?"

Finally.

"But she's not an animal." Bray protested.

"He's right. I haven't ever sprouted a tail or ears or fur." Vixen spoke up just to keep the voice from offering an opinion.

"They don't teach you wolves anything, do they?" Roose sighed and shook his head. "There are two types of latents. The more common latent is the one where the animal never appears. It's a passenger. A latent is usually the result of a human woman and a male shifter, but sometimes it's the other way. They're no different from any other human, except other shifters will recognize there's an animal hiding inside of them. No one knows how or why it happens, but since the animal doesn't affect anything, it's a non-issue.

"And then there's the second latent. The animal isn't satisfied with being a passenger. It wants more and is stronger than its counterpart. There's not a good explanation for how it happens, but somehow the animal fuses with the man, or woman. They're one entity. I haven't heard of one speaking to the body they inhabit, but they help them in other ways. Giving them most of the heightened abilities of the animal and urging them to act in stressful situations."

Vixen bobbed her head up and down along with Roose's explanation. It explained everything. It also scared the hell out of her. She shot to her feet and headed out the front door. "Excuse me."

Bray stood and started to follow.

Roose stopped him with a few words. "She needs time. Give it to her."

Vixen closed the door behind her and plopped her bottom on the front steps. She leaned back against her elbows and stared up at the blue sky through the canopy of the leaves.

See. Friend.

"Who's a friend?" Vixen didn't know how else to talk to the voice. She figured she could think her words, but that meant the voice was privy to her thoughts. Something she didn't want to consider.

All of us. Bear. Wolf. Mate. Coyote. Me.

"You? What are you?"

I don't know.

CHAPTER ELEVEN

AS VIXEN walked into the yard, Allard stood at the edge of the woods, staring off at nothing. He raised an arm and waved, but kept his back to her. He wouldn't have been able to see her approach, so he must have heard it. Interesting.

She crossed the open yard and stood next to Allard, staring off at the same nothing. "Anything exciting?"

Allard shook his head. "Bray not with you?"

"You can't tell?" She was genuinely curious.

"Sensed someone was there. We don't get many strangers out here, so figured it was someone I knew."

Vixen nodded, even though Allard wasn't looking at her and couldn't see the gesture.

"Kinda surprised Bray let you walk alone in the woods though."

"He gets protective?"

"Protective?" Allard let out a loud laugh. "Bray's a control freak. We're old enough to make our own decisions, but his wolf won't let us."

"Because he's sure you'll end up fighting one another if left to your own devices." Vixen stuck her hands in the deep pockets of the loose fitting jeans and leaned against a nearby tree. "If any of the others told you to do something, would you?"

"Hell no."

"But you listen when Bray tells you. Why?"

"He's the Alpha."

"Maybe, if you gave him a reason not to give orders, he'd leave you on your own. Ever try doing what he expects before he has to ask?" Vixen had similar conversations with young soldiers who hadn't fully gotten over their resentment of the perceived privileges of commanding officers. What they almost always failed to realize was that along with the privileges came a load of responsibility. It was one of the reasons Vixen liked what she did. She didn't worry that her orders could end someone's life.

"Not sure why you care. It's not like you're one of us. Or even part of our pack." Allard turned and walked into the house.

Sad.

"What?" She hated talking to herself, but hated thinking her half of the conversation more.

Allard. Sad.

"Why?" Vixen leaned against the tree and looked across the yard at the empty porch.

Not sure. Ask him.

"Yeah, sure. I'll get right on that."

"Right on what?" Bray stepped out from behind her.

"Nothing." Vixen wished she could have said his appearance surprised her, but she wasn't. The voice hadn't alerted her, but she had expected him to show, eventually. Allard had been right. Bray would never let her traipse through the woods on her own. He had given her space, though. "Thanks, by the way."

Bray ducked his chin in acknowledgment. "Should thank Roose. He kept me from chasing after you."

"You or the wolf?" Vixen figured a lot of what drove these men was the animal inside of them. If what Roose said was even halfway true, whatever was inside of her also drove her. At least her voice had been subtle until recently.

"Wolf." Bray reached over and took her hand.

She should have pulled away, but since she was probably leaving in the morning, it didn't hurt to give him the moment. "Do you think it's true? What Roose said?"

"It explains a lot. Just because I believed it was a legend, doesn't mean it's impossible."

"So it's also possible I have a brain tumor. I've heard about these things happening. Someone gets a tumor and they hear voices and it changes them."

"Tumors don't heal bullet wounds." Bray was a spoilsport.

"My voice. It doesn't know what it is. I might really be certifiable."

"You aren't."

Vixen squeezed Bray's hand. "I know."

"We should have a conversation."

Vixen frowned at him. "You mean we haven't already met our quota of conversations we never thought we'd have?"

He stared at the ground and avoided her gaze. "Vi…"

Her cheeks heated, and she bit her bottom lip. A male using a nickname shouldn't cause a reaction, but the timbre of Bray's voice did things to her body she had long outgrown.

"You don't have to decide now. Or even soon. But you need to give me some warning before you leave. I need to keep my wolf in check, but I also have to keep the pack in line."

"I'll probably leave in the morning." Her hand slipped from his, but he kept their fingers hooked together.

Liar.

In her mind, Vixen stuck her tongue out at the invisible voice.

"Just give me enough time to prepare or my wolf is liable to hunt you down and I doubt Roose will be able to stop him."

Vixen lifted her chin in an approximation of a nod. "I can do that."

Bray tugged her along to the front porch. "Come on. Let's check on any damage the boys might have contributed to. Then we'll decide what they should make for dinner."

"They cook? Aren't you scared they'll burn the house down?"

"It hasn't happened yet." He looked over his shoulder and grinned at her. "Roose is coming over later since we didn't exactly finish our conversation. Plus, with Roose here, the boys won't get into too much trouble."

"Why is that?"

Bray stopped and spun to face her. He used his free hand to rub his knuckles against her sternum. "You felt it. You might not understand what it was, but you could feel it here, right?"

"The heaviness?"

"Yeah, but imagine, Vi, that weight pushing not just on you, but on something inside you as well?"

There was that nickname again. If she wasn't probably leaving in the morning, she'd ask him to stop. "It didn't cause you any discomfort?"

"Nope. My wolf is more than capable of pushing back. Roose isn't more dominant than me, but his animal is bigger. When it comes to the boys, their wolves are dominant, but not strong enough to face down Roose and win."

"It's like an invisible nature documentary."

Bray chuckled and pulled her in close for a quick hug before resuming their trek back to the house. "That it is."

He hadn't released her hand, but she didn't say anything. After all, she was probably leaving in the morning.

CHAPTER TWELVE

"TEVIN, stop taking the plates off the table." Vixen glared at the young man as he followed behind Finley, scooping up the plates, bowls, and cups with his name on them.

"But they're mine..."

Allard snatched a plate from Tevin's hands and licked it. "Now it's mine."

"Children, all of you. You're no better than preschoolers." Vixen tried not to laugh at their antics.

Jackson entered the kitchen and sat at the table. "You spend time around children?"

"Me? Nope. Well, not intentionally." Vixen took the plate from Allard and washed it in the sink before handing it back to Finley. Maybe she could distract them enough to get the table set with no more attempts to mark things.

"Do you want children?" Tevin paused his gathering of signed dinnerware to ask his question.

"Not particularly, no." Vixen dried her hands on a towel. She faced the table and leaned against the sink. "Plus, the older you are, the more risks there are. Not to mention what I've gone through. I'm not even sure I can have them."

"So you don't want any pups?" Tevin asked again.

"Pups?"

"Well, yeah, you and Bray last night. And pretty sure this morning too. So are pups next?" Finley added to her growing embarrassment.

Tevin thrust his hips back and forth while Finley mimicked a female moaning. Bray, who had slipped into the kitchen, slapped both boys on the back of their heads. "Enough."

The boys switched roles. Finley added hand gestures to his thrusts, and Tevin included masculine grunts between the high-pitched moans. Vixen couldn't say it was an improvement, but she gave them high marks for effort.

She pointed to the large pan filled with sliced mushrooms and lifted an eyebrow at Finley. "They'll burn."

Over the years, Vixen had perfected the ability of issuing an order that sounded like a suggestion. Finley, having gone through basic training at least, had been primed to obey those suggestions without questioning the reason for them. If she had hinted to any of the others, they should stir the mushrooms before they burned, they would have wanted to know why she didn't pick a spoon.

The distraction was enough to stop the lewd gestures, and Bray didn't have to hit them anymore. A win-win for everyone.

"She doesn't need pups, not with you idiots." Bray watched her from across the room with a satisfied smile teasing at his lips.

His gaze lowered to her stomach, a stomach she worked hard to keep flat. Not because of vanity, but because fitness played a significant role in increasing her life expectancy from minutes to months. She liked months. If he was imagining her carrying a child, she needed to nip that little fantasy in the bud. Besides, she was probably leaving tomorrow night.

"To answer the question you asked, Tevin, no, I don't want children." She looked around the kitchen, expecting a blast of questions asking why not, but none came. Vixen changed the subject into what she thought was safe territory. "Where's Leighton?"

The young males looked around the kitchen, noticing Leighton's absence for the first time.

Bray pushed off the wall and crossed to the fridge. He took out two bottles of beer, held them in one hand and reached his other hand out to her. "Come on, the boys can finish getting dinner ready."

Vixen took his hand and allowed him to lead her through the house and out the front to the porch where they both settled on the swing. Bray opened the beers and handed her a bottle.

After several minutes of sipping and swinging in silence, Vixen squinted out at the woods. "You bring me out here for a reason or just to enjoy the view?"

"Leighton's a good kid, but his wolf has problems and there are days when he needs to go off on his own. He doesn't trust his wolf, and I do my best to respect that."

"Is that why he wasn't part of the fighting this morning?"

"I think he wanted to impress you more than keeping the others safe. Leighton has no problem letting his wolf out for a good brawl and can hold his own. There are just times when he needs to be alone." Bray stretched his arm along the back of the swing and brushed his fingers over her shoulder. "How are your wounds?"

Vixen's thoughts halted mid-stream and backtracked to consider Bray's question. She shifted her weight, putting pressure on her hip, and rolled her shoulder. The reminder of an ache was present, but this was what she expected after weeks of recovery, not a day. "Better. A lot better. Do you heal this fast?"

Bray grinned at her, and the giddiness of a school girl invaded her body. Damn, but Bray did a good job of reminding Vixen she was a woman. "You saw the marks on the boys after the fight. Did you see any marks when you were in the kitchen?"

Now that Bray brought it up, she didn't notice any marks or even the stiffness that came from using muscles. "Ever been shot?"

"Yeah." Bray didn't expand on his answer and Vixen enjoyed her own privacy enough not to ask further.

Early summer was always her favorite time of year, though she rarely got to enjoy it. She couldn't have chosen a better place to retire, although she preferred a golden parachute instead of a golden bullet with her actual retirement. Vixen stretched her legs out in front of her and leaned back in the swing. If she angled her body so she was closer to Bray, it was by accident.

As the sun set, Bray tapped her shoulder and lifted his chin toward the woods. "Here he comes."

She didn't see anything or anyone in the distance. "Who?"

"Leighton." Bray slid her closer to him. He did that around the younger males. She figured it was one of those wolf things.

It didn't bother her when he coddled and petted her. Or maybe it bothered her and her voice distracted her. But that gave her voice too much credit. And then her eyes found what Bray saw. In the gray light of dusk, a dark shadow emerged from the tree-line across the large yard.

"You keep the yard clear of trees so no one can sneak up on you, don't you?" Vixen asked as Leighton loped across the long grass toward the house.

"It makes it more difficult for someone to knock on the door without us knowing. Doesn't mean it doesn't happen occasionally, but it's rare." Bray studied Leighton's approach with unblinking eyes. "Have a good run?"

Leighton climbed up the steps and stood in front of both Vixen and Bray, shifting his weight from foot to foot, but didn't answer Bray's question right away. Keeping his eyes lowered, he raised his chin and bared his throat, not to Bray, but to Vixen.

Bray leaned his head toward Vixen's and narrowed his eyes.

She witnessed the young males perform the same gesture to Bray, especially when he issued them an order. The behavior was all wolf. Like last night, when she was with Bray, this felt big. Leighton's act was important, and she didn't need the voice to translate the significance.

Smart girl.

Vixen ignored the voice. Leighton deserved that much from her, at least.

When she'd seen the boys bare their necks to Bray, he'd stared at them for a few seconds before giving them a quick nod and continuing on with whatever he had been doing. She did her best to copy Bray with the same curt nod, but instead of continuing her conversation with Bray and ignoring Leighton, she included him.

"The others are inside getting dinner ready."

Leighton's body rocked from side to side, as though man and wolf were at odds with one another. Finally, after what felt like an eternity, but was only seconds, Leighton reached behind him. When he brought his hand back in front, he held a knife with the hilt toward her.

Her knife.

Unbelievable. Leighton found her knife. She thought for sure it had been lost.

Vixen reached out and held her hand palm up. Leighton set the NSW-Dagger in her hand. Her fingers wrapped around the black micarta handle and she welcomed its warmth.

"Could you teach me?"

She looked up from the double-edged dagger and studied the young man in front of her. He didn't like maintaining eye contact, but wasn't willing to look away from her. As though that would influence her decision. When he met her gaze, a need hid behind his bright green eyes. Vixen understood that need.

"Of course. Tomorrow morning?"

Leighton gave her a nod and a small smile, then after a few seconds headed inside.

"Does that mean you're not leaving tomorrow?" Bray asked.

"It means I'm probably leaving the day after tomorrow."

Liar.

From the look Bray gave her, he agreed with the voice. But at least he kept quiet.

CHAPTER THIRTEEN

ONE day turned to two. Two days turned to three. Then, before Vixen realized it, a week had passed, and she was still living with the Broken Peak Pack. She spent her mornings training Leighton with the dagger, her afternoons working with the rest of the boys, and her evenings after dinner with Bray.

While the boys spent their evenings finding ways to maim each other for fun, Vixen and Bray stayed as far from the stupid antics of youth as possible. Every night, before falling asleep, Vixen kissed Bray goodnight and told him she was probably leaving in the morning. The voice had long since stopped calling her a liar and Bray no longer bothered rolling his eyes.

But this evening was different. Instead of sending the boys out after dinner, he made them clean up. Vixen's training must have worn the boys down, because none of them questioned the directive. He grabbed the jug of pawpaw shine in one hand, Vixen's hand with the other, and took them both out to the porch. He settled her on the swing and tucked a blanket around her legs before sitting down next to her.

"So..." Bray broke the silence after a few minutes.

"So?" Vixen had an idea where the conversation was headed, but Bray was fun to poke at. Not as much fun to poke at as Roose, because who didn't love to poke a bear, but Bray was a close second.

"You're still here."

Vixen smiled and took a swig from the jug. The first night she tried the moonshine, she thought she died. And the following morning, she wished she had. The stuff was potent, illegal, and able to melt seven layers of paint off an old house.

She was going to make Bray work for the answers he wanted. "I am."

"No one's showed up looking for you or your body. And Garreth hasn't heard about anyone snooping around War who doesn't belong."

"It's only been a week." Vixen sighed and burrowed up against his side. "Where did you and Leighton go this afternoon?"

"We went for a run. His wolf likes to be alone, but he needs to remember he's still part of a pack." Bray kissed the top of her head. "Vi, I said you needed to give me some time before you left so I could prepare my wolf. I'm not sure that's true anymore. I might not have made the mating official so that every other shifter knows you're mine, but you are his."

Vixen wrapped her arms around his middle and tucked her legs underneath her. "Do you wish you hadn't found me?"

"No. I wish I killed the men who shot you."

Well. Okay, then. Both Vixen and her voice liked his answer. A lot.

"You know what I wish? I wish I met you, not because you found me half dead, but because I found you. And I wish the General was still healthy. I would have liked to introduce you to him."

"Who's the General, Vi?" He twirled the end of her braid around his fingers.

"He's my Mac. Except he doesn't have an illegal still." She picked up the jug from where Bray had set it on the ground and took a long swallow before placing it back down. "But he had a heart attack, and they forced him to retire. And then they ordered my retirement. If the General was still active, he would have protected me. Or at the very least helped me fake my death so I could retire in relative peace."

"My parents would like you. Especially my father."

Vixen tilted her head back and looked up at Bray's chin. "You have parents?"

"Yes, I have parents. I didn't hatch from an egg."

"But your Alpha kicked you out?"

"I have a dominant wolf, Vi. A very dominant wolf. If I stayed with my parents' pack, I would have challenged the Alpha when I was young and caused a riff. He didn't send me away as punishment. He sent me away because he had to do what was best for the pack."

"Do you see your parents still?"

"Yeah. They come out and visit. It's for the best considering there's a strong possibility the boys would destroy the house if I left them alone for a week. Hell, I don't think the house would still be standing after a single day. I want my parents to meet you, Vi. I want them to know I found you. AND I WANT TO MEET THIS GENERAL."

"I should have left a week ago." Vixen whispered to no one.

"But you didn't." Bray's chest vibrated with a low growl.

"But I didn't."

She was never supposed to stay. Staying with the pack would increase their chance of discovery. Even if she wasn't here, the risk of someone looking for her corpse and stumbling across Bray or one of the boys didn't go away. But this place, more than anything else in her life, felt like home. She'd never called any place home after they recruited her. It was easier not to get attached. This was different. Bray was here, and she couldn't bring him with her if she left.

And what about Leighton? Or the others?

Vixen had no idea what she should do. And not knowing unsettled her. "What am I supposed to do, Bray?"

"I can't tell you that. You have to decide on your own."

She was tired of the conversation. Vixen crawled into Bray's lap and straddled his hips. She didn't care who heard or saw, all she wanted was to feel.

Apparently Bray wanted that too, because he pressed his hands against her cheeks and brought her face closer to his until all she could see was the deep brown of his eyes flecked with gold.

Bray didn't hesitate or soften his approach, he just consumed. And Vixen went along for the ride. She parted her lips for him and welcomed his exploring tongue and soft lips. While he kept her mouth occupied, Bray unbuttoned her shirt and slipped it down her arms. She dragged her fingertips down his chest, feeling his muscles flex beneath the soft fabric of his thin flannel, before working on unfastening the button and fly of his old jeans.

With a gentle bite to her bottom lip, he dropped his mouth to her bare breasts and lashed her tight nipples with the tip of his tongue before wrapping his lips around one and sucking on the hard bud then switching to the other breast. He sucked hard, and it was almost enough to send her over the edge. Vixen didn't want him to stop and pressed his head to her breasts when he made to pull his mouth away from her.

Whatever he was doing to her breasts sent a line of pleasure directly between her legs. She reached into his jeans and freed his cock, wrapping her hand around the thick girth then sliding her palm up and down his hard length. Bray slipped his hand down the front of her jeans, easy to do since they were so loose, and cupped her pussy. His thumb pressed against her clit, circling it to add to the pleasure his mouth gave her.

Vixen needed more. And so did Bray. He didn't bother unbuttoning her jeans. He yanked them down past her hips until the head of his cock rubbed against her clit. She worked a leg free from the jeans and lifted herself up over his hips. With her hand still on his cock, she guided him into her. Keeping her eyes locked on his, Vixen didn't move slowly to give her body time to stretch to his size. She dropped down fast and hard, taking his full size completely.

The sharp pinch of pain was exquisite, and her head fell back as she screamed out in pleasure.

Vixen dug her fingers into his shoulders. Bray's fingers bit into her hips. Together they moved. His cock hit all the right nerve endings and her pussy fluttered around him, rewarding him for the pleasure he delivered.

Bray's hips bucked hard, and his body quivered. He was close, but he held himself back.

Her orgasm was close as she danced nearer to the edge. Vixen didn't beg, but she didn't know how else to convey the level of her need to him. She wasn't going to find her release alone. She needed him to come with her. But she didn't just need her release. She needed Bray to take all her excuses away. He wouldn't though. Not unless she asked him. "Bray…"

"I have you, Vi, but not like this. Not here. Not now." He gritted out the words between clenched teeth, barely holding onto the thin tether of control.

But he didn't have her. Not the way his wolf wanted and not the way she wanted.

His body stiffened as every muscle tightened and his cock grew. With a shout, Bray exploded inside of her with a hard thrust up as he pulled her down hard on him.

She screamed out his name to the moon as her orgasm chased after his and didn't stop.

Seconds, or maybe it was minutes, later, Bray wrapped his arm around her and pulled her closer to him. Taking the blanket, he wrapped it around her and held her against him. She tucked her head under his chin as they both relaxed in the pleasant aftershocks of an intense bout of sex that might have made the ground shake.

"I want to tell you not to go, Vi. But I can't. So, I'll say what I can. I don't want you to leave. I want you to stay." He pressed his lips against her forehead.

Bray filled her so completely, and Vixen fit against him perfectly. As though they were made for each other.

Finally.

"I'm not leaving." She kissed his chest before pressing her cheek against him so she heard his heartbeat to the same rhythm as her own. "I want to stay here. With you."

CHAPTER FOURTEEN

THUMP-thump-thump-thump-thump. Vixen's eyes snapped open, and she slid out of bed. She couldn't afford to wake up Bray. Her first priority was silence.

Thump-thump-thump-thump-thump.

Jeans and shirt. She wished she still had her thick tactical clothing, but what she had was better than nothing.

Boots. Her own boots. At least she wouldn't be barefoot.

Thump-thump-thump-thump-thump.

Dagger. It wouldn't be much help at first, but she couldn't face them unarmed.

Thump-thump-thump-thump-thump.

She should have left a week ago. She should have left the morning after Bray stitched her up. But she didn't.

And now they found her.

Thump-thump-thump-thump-thump.

With a final look over her shoulder at Bray, thankfully still asleep, Vixen slipped out of the room. She blew him a kiss. It was all she could afford.

WAIT UNTIL THE TEAM REPELLED down before revealing herself, or face them down and lead them away? Away from Bray and his pack.

Bray's survival outweighed her need to take down as many of the team as possible. With a snarl that made the voice proud, Vixen trotted out to the middle of the open yard and stood with her feet shoulder width apart. She stared up at the sound of the approaching helicopter. A modified MD500E. She'd been in enough of them to recognize the sound of their blades cutting through the air.

At least Bray hadn't mated her. His wolf would survive after they finished what the first team failed to do.

She expected a protest, but the voice remained silent.

Vixen waited.

Pop.

She heard the bullet before the burning metal pierced her flesh just to the left of the middle of her chest.

Cowards.

They couldn't even face her. They used a sniper instead.

But they didn't trust the sniper. That was their weakness. The MD500E's doors were open, and the pilot got too close. She didn't have a gun, but she had her dagger.

Vixen was a killer. She did bad things to bad people, so good people could live good lives.

The pack was good.

The men sent to kill her were bad.

She shouldn't still be alive, but she was.

And Vixen was prepared to take advantage of it.

Her feet moved, pounding against the ground.

The pilot must have thought the sniper missed, because he lowered the helicopter and angled the nose away. An opportunity for a second shot. The pilot took a chance with the low pass. But Vixen was ready. The dagger left her hand and cartwheeled through the air in a perfect arc.

A last resort.

A one in a million chance.

Vixen learned to believe in the impossible this past week. She had faith she would witness one more impossibility before she died.

The dagger missed the intended mark, the pilot's right eye, but it still hit his shoulder. The pilot couldn't recover from the low pass with the pain and shock of the blade penetrating his flesh.

Too low to the ground.

Too many trees.

Too high altitude.

Too confident.

All of it added together into a recipe for a disaster. But underestimating Vixen was the pilot's true downfall.

Vixen collapsed as the helicopter crumpled to the ground and went tail over nose a few times before coming to a stop at the base of the mountain, far enough away from the house to keep it safe from the fiery ball of crumpled metal.

As the ground met Vixen's body, she wished for one thing. She didn't want to die alone.

You aren't alone. You've never been alone.

CHAPTER FIFTEEN

THE sound of a gunshot cutting through the silence of the night woke Bray. Normally, he would have stopped and assessed the situation. When he didn't find Vixen in bed with him, he leapt to his feet, not even bothering to get dressed. He grabbed a pair of jeans and ran for the front door. He barely pulled them up as he skidded to a halt in the wet grass of the yard.

The burning helicopter went unnoticed.

The screaming men went ignored.

All Bray saw as he stood in the middle of the chaos surrounding him was the fallen body fifty feet in front of him. His wolf didn't need to scent the air to know it held blood. Her blood.

The screams called to his wolf. He would rip out the throats and disembowel the men who did this to her. They would die for what they did.

Eventually.

His wolf urged him on, pushing at him to let the beast out to destroy those who stole the life from his mate.

Bray looked up at the sky, ready to let his wolf free, but he needed to see Vixen first. He already knew what he would find. But Bray needed to say goodbye to the woman he should have told he loved before he surrendered control of the men's fate to the monster inside of him pleading for release.

Vixen's face was turned to the house, as though she had been looking for him. With each step closer, his wolf tore at him from inside. The wolf could wait. The woman couldn't. Bray fell to his knees and held her outstretched hand between his two large palms. She wasn't small, by any means, but her hand looked tiny compared to his. Her skin was still warm, and he vowed not to let go. Not until Mac or Roose pulled him away from her.

He bent forward and pressed his lips to her forehead. He should have been there for her. Bray sat up and stared down at her. Her eyes were open, and he knew he should have closed them, but he couldn't do it. He wanted to remember that exact shade of beautiful green for the rest of his life.

As he stared down at her, Vixen's eyes glowed bright green.

It had to be the moon. Right?

Cradling her cheek in his palm, Bray turned her head so she looked up at the sky. He knelt over her, shielding the moonlight with his broad shoulders. They still glowed.

Impossible.

The surrounding chaos wasn't just ignored. Bray forgot about everything. The explosion. The helicopter. The men. His pack would take care of that. Vixen and Bray were all that existed at the base of Broken Peak Mountain.

She didn't have an animal, not like the others. If she had been the latent Roose and Mac believed, her animal wouldn't be capable of revealing herself in Vixen's eyes.

The glow flared brightly before fading slightly, but it didn't go away.

"Let your wolf claim her!" The shout came from the woods. Both Mac and Roose screamed as they barreled through the trees, not caring about the destruction they encountered.

"What?" Bray refused to look away from the women he had unknowingly pulled into his arms.

"Claim her, you idiot. And do it now!" Roose bellowed as he approached Bray.

"Let your wolf out and let him claim her." Mac stumbled to a halt a few feet away.

"What the hell are you talking about?" Claiming a nearly dead female would be no different from Bray committing suicide.

"We were wrong. Her animal isn't latent." Roose pressed his hands down on his knees and bent forward as he regained his breath. When he looked up, his eyes glowed bright silver. His bear was close. "You can save her, but you need to claim her. Now."

"If you don't, Roose will." Mac growled, pacing anxiously behind the bear shifter. "But we don't got much time. So man up and let your wolf out or back off and let Roose handle it."

Bray cut off further comments with a sharp stare at Roose. "Are you sure?"

"No. But I know it's the only chance you have."

The words Roose spoke were enough. Before Bray contemplated the pure stupidity of claiming Vixen after he let his wolf out, he slipped his jeans off then slid back inside of himself and allowed his wolf to burst free.

The massive wolf stood over Vixen, planting his paws around her so his body shielded hers. Bray didn't have to communicate anything to the wolf. The beast dropped his head, bared his teeth, and clamped down on the fleshy part of Vixen's shoulder.

Bray watched it all from behind the wolf's eyes. After several seconds, he pushed the wolf to release her, but the wolf refused to let go. The monster was waiting for something and fought against Bray, taking back control. Man and wolf clashed occasionally, but Bray had never had so much trouble wrenching control back from the animal.

"Bray, change man. You need to back the hell off and fast." Roose yelled out, but kept his distance. He wasn't stupid. An Alpha claiming his mate was a danger to any male close by. "If Mac is right, you need to get away from her. She won't have any control."

Between Roose's words and tone, something kicked on in Bray's brain and he dragged the wolf back inside of him. When he came back to himself, he knelt over Vixen, staring down at the torn skin on the base of her neck.

It was bleeding. And it shouldn't have been. Not if she was as close to death as he believed. Bray's gaze traveled from her neck to her eyes. The glow had intensified. Her eyes lit up the dark night, reflecting the golden amber from the flames of the crash.

"Back off." Mac growled.

Bray didn't need to be told twice. He scrambled off Vixen and backed away from her. Since her arrival, big things had happened at Broken Peak that Bray never believed would happen, like finding his mate. Whatever was happening was another one of those big things Vixen seemed to have brought with her.

He wanted to reach out and take Vixen's hand, but the long growl rolling out of her stopped him. Bray yanked up his jeans and stood between Mac and Roose. "What's happening?"

"A legend is being born." Mac's voice held only reverence. The panic and hint of fear faded away, as though he never doubted what was about to happen.

Vixen's glowing gaze turned to the three males standing by her, and she blinked slowly. Her eyes didn't just glow, they had changed. The pair of eyes staring up at them didn't belong to Vixen, they belonged to a raptor.

But raptors didn't growl. They screamed. A terrifying sound that instilled fear in those they hunted.

"What the..." Roose saw it too.

"Watch."

Vixen sat up, her head cocked to the side. Her head jerked down, and she looked at the red stain that flowered on her shirt.

"Thank you." The voice that came out of Vixen's mouth didn't belong to her. It was still feminine, but nothing like the sultry purr Bray had come to enjoy. With slow jerky movements, Vixen stood, as though she wasn't used to the arms and legs she controlled.

"Mac..." Bray hissed out.

"Just watch. Nothing else we can do."

Vixen's mouth pulled back in an approximation of a grin. Apparently she agreed with Mac. Her head cocked to the other side and those glowing eyes focused on the helicopter. More specifically, on the males pulling the soldiers from the burning crash.

"Oh, shit..." Bray jogged toward the crash. He had no idea what was about to happen, but whatever it was didn't bode well for those who got between whatever Vixen had become and her goal. "Jackson, get the hell away from there!"

The young males looked up and didn't even question Bray's order. They scattered off, far away from the crash. He felt the wave of power pulsate behind him and realized they hadn't moved because of his order, but because of that power. Bray stopped and turned.

Vixen stalked towards him, stripping her clothes as she moved.

"Mac..." Bray's breath caught in his throat. The bullet wound was gone and the mating mark had scarred. Most shifters took days to heal, Vixen healed in minutes.

"I see it."

"Not yet, but you will." Vixen corrected Mac.

Most first shifts took a long time. In the worst cases, the Alpha had to pull the animal out. But Vixen didn't have that problem. Her animal burst free as though she'd been shifting her entire life.

Only her animal wasn't the raptor Bray expected. Well, not entirely. Her animal might have had the beak and wings of a bird of prey, but she also had the body of a lion.

Mac had been right. A legend had been born that night. Vixen wasn't just any shifter, she was a mythical beast come to life.

Vixen was a griffin.

She almost died, was claimed, and became a beautiful pure white griffin in one night.

Her wings, stretched out from between her shoulders, spanned at least twelve feet across. From toe to ear, she stood close to five feet. With ebony claws at least three inches long and a formidable hooked beak, also black, Vixen wasn't dangerous. She was deadly. And she wanted the men who hurt her.

CHAPTER SIXTEEN

THE slightest movement not only registered in Vixen's mind, but caught her immediate attention. Within seconds, she had assessed and identified the sources of the movement into simple classifications.

Friend.

Foe.

Food.

Apparently both friend and foe qualified for food, something the woman lurking inside the beast found unnerving. However, none of that matched the shock and pain of a monster ripping out of her body.

When she faded into the darkness of unconsciousness and what she assumed would eventually be her death, the voice refused to let Vixen give up. The voice had demanded Vixen's attention. Then Bray found her and bit her.

The bite was the key. She understood that. Well, no, she didn't understand the claiming bite freeing the animal, but she understood the pure satisfaction that rolled through her body as soon as the wolf's teeth broke through her skin and sunk into her flesh.

She stood, but that was the voice's doing, not hers. The voice was also the driving force to reach the men who hurt her. She hadn't taken more than a few steps before she folded inside of herself while the animal broke out of her. Vixen didn't cause the change. It was all the voice. The voice controlled everything.

More movement across the yard.

Stupid men. Foe. Food.

The massive paws swallowed the distance across the yard to the broken machine with the men crawling out of it.

"Vixen!" Bray's shout carried across the yard, but she didn't slow.

The men caused this. The men needed to be punished. They had to die.

She neared her goal, the urge to destroy those who caused her harm greater than the urge to listen to Bray's command.

And then she wasn't running alone. Wolves ran with her. Six of them. A bear roared out and the weight of his paws landing against the ground shook the earth. And finally, a coyote wove through the legs of the larger beasts, racing to catch up with the monster in the lead.

The wiry coyote charged in front of her with a burst of speed. He would have tripped her up if her paws hadn't lifted from the ground. With a few solid pumps of her wings, Vixen flew a few feet above the others. Flying was more awkward than running on four feet, but after a few near falls, she learned to trust the wings.

The men saw her approach. A few screamed, but they all ran. Or tried to.

Vixen dove for the nearest man. Hadn't he heard the old saying to run faster than the person in front of him?

She landed on his back, pushing him to the ground as her beak crunched down on the top of his spine.

Good kill. Clean kill.

She looked up, spotting her next target. Before she took flight, the bear charged her. He lowered his head and rammed into her side, knocking her to the ground. She tumbled over, tucking her wings so no harm came to them.

Bad bear.

Vixen pushed back to her paws and faced the bear with a scream of outrage. "No! Mine!"

The others skidded to a stop, circling her. She didn't understand why they blocked her from her goal.

She stretched her wings and pumped them while jumping up, but a wolf leapt for her shoulder, pushing her back to the ground. They worked together, keeping her from taking flight. Without flight, she couldn't reach the men. She couldn't punish them.

The black wolf faced her with legs splayed and growled. Not the nice possessive growl of a satisfied male, but the commanding growl of an angry Alpha.

Alpha?

No.

Vixen didn't have an Alpha.

Vixen wasn't a wolf.

Vixen was a...

Monster.

Vixen wasn't a good woman, but that didn't make her a monster. She had ethics. Everyone she killed deserved death. The team sent to kill her deserved death, but not like this. Not at the claws of a beast who saw them as nothing more than food.

She crumpled to the ground and pulled the monster inside of her. The monster didn't want to hide again and resisted, but Vixen fought back. Vixen didn't know if the change hurt because of the change or because the monster struggled against it. The sticky warmth from the blood of her kill coated her arms and the slick taste of iron coated her tongue.

Bray, the wolf, circled her, keeping the others from getting too close.

Behind her, Finley and Jackson spoke in hushed voices, but her ears picked up every syllable.

"Is that his spine?"

"Yep. And there's his kidney."

"How do you know what a kidney looks like?"

"Well, it looks like a bean and it's kinda reddish." Tevin offered in support of Jackson's claim.

"Pretty sure that's his liver and not his kidney." Allard joined the conversation.

Oh, God, what had she done?

The naked men and black wolf surrounding her didn't register. Vixen only saw the sad brown eyes of the wolf. Until she looked up. Then she spotted Leighton's clear blue eyes watching her. From a safe distance.

She hoped, maybe even wished, for a smile from him. What she received instead was a furrowed brow as he stared at what she had become.

"Leighton?"

He stood silently with his arms crossed over his chest.

She couldn't take it. Every kill before had been good. Targets she researched and judged according to a rigid set of standards she established for her own well-being of mind. The man she killed, correction, the man the monster inside her killed, didn't have the chance to be judged. She didn't doubt she would have found the killing justified, but in her mind that didn't excuse it.

A shower. She needed to wash away the stains. Vixen stood on shaking legs and ran for the house. It wasn't fair to leave the others to deal with the aftermath, but she couldn't stay without losing what little was left of her mind.

Barreling into the house, she bounced off the walls and against the doors into Bray's room. Straight into the shower. She turned on the water as hot as possible and stood under the spray of cold water, not bothering to wait for it to warm.

"You're beautiful, Vi. All of you." The shower still hadn't warmed up when Bray's voice carried through the sound of the water pelting down on the tiles.

"No." Vixen stared at the red water circling down the drain. "Not after tonight. What I did out there…"

Bray stepped into the shower with her and wrapped his arms around her middle while pulling her body flush back against his. "My mate is magnificent."

He turned her so she faced him, but she kept her gaze on the floor so he wouldn't see her crying. Vixen saw the sadness in his wolf's eyes and seeing the same sadness in Bray's eyes would destroy what was left of her.

"Vi, your animal is…"

"A monster."

"A miracle. You're a griffin, Vi, and as far as we know, you're the first and only one of your kind. She's gorgeous, Vi. She's powerful and strong. Hell, you had three dominant males, all Alphas, unable to pull her back. You aren't a monster. You are a protector. A sentinel."

She dared to look at him, not caring if he saw the tears. "But what I did… and you and Leighton…"

He pressed his lips to her forehead, then kissed away the tears. "Not sad about what you did, Vi. I was sad you found your animal the way you did. Thinking you were alone like that and the way she burst from you. But, baby, you pulled her back. First shifts for everyone are difficult, and the Alpha usually has to help with the change. Not with you, Vi."

The water finally warmed up. Bray reached for the soap and lathered her body. When he finished washing her body, he washed her hair. Once he was satisfied, Bray turned the water off and reached for a towel. She stood still while he patted her dry, then wrapped the towel around her body before briskly drying himself off. Bray took her hand and led her into the bedroom.

"We don't have much time."

Vixen's voice, or monster, remained silent. Probably because she was as confused as Vixen. She wouldn't be able to rely on her voice for help here. Not that Vixen would rely on the voice lurking inside her for a while. "Time for what?"

"To be alone. The pack needs to spend time with you. And it's important they do. Especially since you're their Alpha."

"How can they want me after what I did out there..." Vixen looked out the window. An orange light from the flames glowed in the dark blue night, reminding her of the carnage.

"Nope. We aren't talking about that anymore. And Finley took care of the others. He won't leave any traces."

"They'll send more teams. If I'm not here, they might leave you alone."

Bray sat on the side of the bed and pulled her onto his lap. "If they send more men, we'll handle them the same way. And with your animal, Vi, word will get around the shifter community. She's even capable of speech. The people we have inside will deliver the message. Stay away. Or else."

"Or else what?" In Vixen's experience, the men in command bristled when given ultimatums.

"You're one of us, Vi, and you're my mate. It's official in the eye of the shifters too, I went ahead and claimed you for everyone to see. If they cause you harm, they cause our pack harm, and they cause all shifters harm. We've been quiet and hidden for a long time, but it doesn't mean we haven't been preparing for the day we're revealed to the world." Bray dragged his fingers up her arm and across her back, gently tracing the scars from her past until he reached the fresh scar on her neck. Bray kissed the mark. "When I found you out there, lying on the ground and I thought you were gone, I realized something. You aren't just my mate. I love you, Vixen."

Whoa.

This was a new development. Although, in the scheme of things, this was the least odd thing she had dealt with since, well since Bray found her unconscious and brought her into his home.

You love him too.

Great. She was back.

Tell him.

"No."

Bray's eyebrows shot up so high on his forehead they got lost in his hairline. "No? Pretty sure, it's a yes. Nope. I'm certain it's a yes."

"Not you."

"Yes, me." Bray gestured around the empty room with his free arm. "I'm the only one here."

"No. *Her.*" Vixen tapped her forefinger against her temple.

"Ahh." Recognition registered on Bray's face and in his eyes. "Yeah, that will take getting used to."

She'd have to trust what lived inside her, eventually. While she didn't think letting the animal out in the near future without several safety precautions in place would be wise, the voice–

Animal

"Stop reading my thoughts."

Stop thinking.

Bray watched and listened to the one sided argument with a mixture of amusement and confusion.

Vixen shook her head at his expression and closed her eyes. The animal hadn't given her unsound advice. "She says I love you too. And I do."

"Hey." He placed a finger under her chin and lifted her face, waiting until she opened her eyes before continuing. "She knows you, right? As well as you know you. As much as it galls us, sometimes we have to trust our other half."

"After tonight, trusting her will take some time."

"That's fair, but this was as much a shock to her as it was to you. Imagine spending your life in one room with one window. Then the door opens and the world you only understand through a window is wide open and waiting for you to explore."

Vixen stared at him. "Why do you think she didn't know what animal she was?"

"Probably because she's the only one and you've never seen one. Pictures aren't the same as the real thing and like recognizes like. Our legends say there used to be dragons and griffins. We thought they were fairy tales. But you and your griffin aren't myths. My mate is a mother fuckin' legend." He held her face between his hands and pulled her to him as his lips lightly brushed across hers. Another light brush of his lips before his hands tangled in her hair and he deepened his kiss, then kissed his way along her jaw to her ear. "I want you, Vi, but in about thirty seconds the peanut gallery is going to come rolling into the room."

Bray wasn't wrong. The bedroom door swung open, and the boys took it as an invitation. Five excited young males, an old man with a knowing grin, and a giant with a satisfied smirk, strolled into the room.

"Come on, boys, let's give her a few minutes." Bray smiled and kissed her cheek, then lifted her off his lap and set her back on the bed. He grabbed a pair of jeans from the floor and pulled them up while ushering the others out. "Get dressed and join us in the kitchen."

The last thing Vixen wanted was to be alone, but she appreciated Bray's gesture. The trunk, half-filled with old clothes, waited for her across the room. If she was staying, and let's face it she was, she needed new clothes. Vixen hid a few identities from the government, and the accounts held more than enough money for a new wardrobe. She was an Amazon Prime membership away from having women's clothing and not boys' hand-me-downs. Plus, ordering online had the added benefit of not relying on Bray or the others picking out clothes they'd think she'd like.

In the meantime though, it was a pair of Tevin's old jeans and shirt. In case she wasn't sure they belonged to Tevin, he'd written his name down the leg of the jeans and across the front of the shirt.

Vixen paused at the bedroom door. The boys in the kitchen, and even Roose and Mac, were her family now. For better or worse, when Bray saved her life a second time when he claimed her, he gave her a family. Her fingers brushed the mark, needing the reassurance it was really there.

She must have paused at the door for too long because Bray walked up the hallway toward her. "They're getting impatient."

Vixen brushed the back of her hand across her cheek, wiping away a tear that had escaped from her eye.

"Hey, you okay?" Bray wrapped his arms around her waist and pulled her against him.

"Yeah, I'm okay." Bray had given her more now than everyone else combined in the twenty years before. She was alive and loved. She was with friends. She was with her family. And she had an animal inside of her. An animal more lethal than anything her former employers could send her way. "We're more than okay."

"Come and greet your pack, Alpha." Bray laced his fingers through hers and tugged her along to the kitchen. "The sooner we get this part over with, the faster I can get you back to the bedroom and finish what I didn't even get a chance to start."

Vixen laughed and allowed him to lead her along. She was alive and loved. What more did she need?

TURN THE PAGE FOR *BROKEN HERO* EXTRAS, INCLUDING

The official, Jules Crisare-Sanctioned "What Kind of Shifter are You?" Quiz

An excerpt from the next Broken Peak novel, *BROKEN SAGE*

And More!

THE OFFICIAL "WHAT KIND OF SHIFTER ARE YOU?" QUIZ

You've read Broken Hero and laughed at the antics of the Broken Peak Pack and cheered when Bray claimed Vixen and accidentally on purpose released the Griffin lurking inside of her. Right? I mean maybe you didn't do all those things, but let's just pretend you have. Now, I bet you're wondering where you'd fit in the pack. Would you be a wolf shifter? Or a griffin shifter? Or maybe another kind of shifter entirely. Well, you no longer have to wonder. In the short time it takes you to answer the questions below, you'll find out what kind of shifter you are.

WHAT SHIFTER AM I?

(If you want to find out what kind of shifter your partner is, replace "you" with "he/she/they". Depending on the result, you might want to keep it to yourself.)

1. When Vixen and Bray invite you to a barbecue at Broken Peak, you:

>   a. Hide in the woods and hope no one finds you

>   b. Show up earlier and be the last to leave and drink the most moonshine

2. Vixen asks you to steal a shifter artifact from a private collector who refuses to sell (there's no chance of getting caught), you:

>   a. Tell her no way

>   b. Tell her sure, why not

3. Vixen thinks you should find a mate, you:

>   a. Go out with whoever Mac recommends, and of course they're a perfect match, so you agree.

>   b. Create profiles on shifter-r-us with the rest of Broken Peak Pack and go out on group dates so your friends can give you instant advice. Plus, if they don't like your friends, they aren't for you.

4. War passed a new ordinance, barring all concealed weapons, even daggers, you:

    a. Don't bring the dagger Vixen got for you into town and leave it at home instead

    b. Ignore the ordinance, besides it's not like you go to War all that often

5. After a long day chasing down false alarms that led no where followed by a double dose of training from Vixen, you just want to go home and fall into bed, but your best friend sends a text, asking if you want to go out for dinner in thirty minutes, you:

    a. Call them back right away, since you plan on venting and your best friend is a great listener

    b. Ignore the message and call your friend back the next morning, you plan on spending the night alone with your favorite book

6. While walking through the park late at night with no one around, you see a new "Keep Off Grass" sign, you:

    a. Complain to yourself, but avoid walking on the grass

    b. Yank the sign out, throw it into the trees, then gleefully hop around on the grass since there's no more sign to stop you

ANSWERS

1. a=1, b=0

3. a=0, b=1

4. a=1, b=0

5. a=0, b=1

6. a=1, b=0

Add up your points! Have the number? Great, now if you scored:

0-1 GRIFFIN
Always up for a group hunt or hanging out with the pack, even if it means exploring forbidden territory.

2 WOLF
You take every opportunity to spend time with your friends and pack and always obey your Alpha.

3-4 COYOTE
You don't mind occasionally hanging out with friends, but prefer to spend most of your time alone with yourself and never let something like rules get in the way of doing something.

5-6 BEAR
You're the strong and silent type, always ready to help the few close friends you have as long as you aren't breaking any rules.

AN EXCERPT FROM THE NEXT BROKEN PEAK PACK NOVEL, *BROKEN SAGE*

Jackson is done playing. It's high time to settle down and learn how to alpha. He'll lead his own pack when it's time to leave Broken Peak behind. But when a woman he doesn't remember and a surprise son arrive on their doorstep, his priorities change. Words like "father" and "mate" begin haunting him. So does Eleanor, whose very presence threatens all shifters.

"OI, Mac, what's so important that it can't wait for the morning!" A woman called out from outside the cottage.

Eleanor tripped over herself to get out of the bathroom and in front of Foster before the stranger came inside the cottage. She barely trusted Mac because of Wayne, and that trust tangentially included Roose, but Roose was as far as the transitive property reached. She found Mac watching the door with his head cocked to the side and Foster peering around Mac's shoulder.

"Oh. Well, this is unexpected." The woman stood in the open doorway staring at Foster. She tilted her head forward to get a better look "Yeah, I can see how waiting wasn't an option."

Roose pushed the woman inside and tossed the car keys to Eleanor. "Your car is in a safe spot and I got your bags."

Eleanor barely caught the keys before they dropped to the ground.

"Vixen, this here is Eleanor. And the boy is Foster. Foster and Eleanor, this is Vixen. A friend." Mac leaned back on his couch and grinned. "I expect the others will be along in a few seconds."

If Eleanor went by appearances alone, she'd have grabbed Foster and locked the two of them in the bathroom. Mac might have called Vixen a friend, but the woman had a scary calculating look to her. The only thing keeping Eleanor in place was that Vixen hadn't taken more than a few steps into the room.

Vixen shook her head from side to side and narrowed her eyes at Mac. "I hope you didn't arrange this for entertainment purposes."

Eleanor grinned. Whoever this Vixen was, she had no problem calling out Mac. And from the red flush on Mac's ears, her accusation wasn't off the mark.

"Brace yourself. Things are about to get even more wild." Vixen stepped to the side and pulled Roose with her, leaving the doorway open.

The conversation left Eleanor confused. She didn't understand what anyone was talking about and still didn't understand why Wayne sent her to Mac or how he could help them.

"Damn it, Mac. Vi and I were about to have a nice evening together. This better be good." A dark haired older man, somewhere in his early forties, stepped into the small cottage and came to an abrupt halt as soon as his gaze landed on Foster, "oh."

"That's what I said, Bray," Vixen reached for the man's hand and pulled him to her.

Eleanor stepped closer to the back of the couch and rested her hand on Foster's shoulder.

"Jackson, you're going to want to step inside for a moment." Bray called through the open door.

Jackson?

It couldn't be. What were the chances? Maybe Jackson was a common name for shifters. Eleanor did her best to convince herself that the man Bray called to wasn't the same Jackson her sister named. And it was working too. Her mind rambled through the list of reasons it was impossible. Well, at least until the man walked through the doorway.

Jackson, she assumed, wasn't as big as Roose but close enough for Eleanor to have to tilt her head back to look at his face, had the same color hair as Foster. The same eyes. The same chin and jaw. His forehead even crinkled the same way when he concentrated. At least Eleanor assumed Jackson was concentrating from the way he stared at Foster.

Eleanor stepped around the couch, plopped down on the cushions, and pulled Foster into her lap. She wrapped her arms around him and pulled him tight against her body.

Jackson's mouth dropped. He stepped back until his body pressed against the wall. Eleanor recognized the shock. She'd experienced it several times over since Foster came into her life.

"Mac?" Jackson's voice shook. Whether from fear or anger, Eleanor didn't know.

Foster looked at the three unknown faces and smiled. "Are you friends with Doctor Ritchie? I am too. So that makes us friends."

"That's one way to put it." Vixen smiled, but kept her gaze on Jackson.

Jackson stood still and silent. The only movement came from his blinking eyes and the opening and closing of his mouth. As though he wanted to say something, but couldn't form the words.

Foster squirmed in an attempt to wriggle free, but Eleanor was prepared for the move and tightened her arms.

Mac cleared his throat and stood. "Wayne called me. Asked if I could help a friend out. Seems there was a bit of a kerfluffle back in Missouri and Foster and his mom need a place to stay for a while."

"Mac," Jackson's voice still shook, but this time Eleanor knew it was from anger.

"Your questions can wait, Jackson." Mac trampled over Jackson's words. "Now, Eleanor needs a place to stay. Roose and I don't have much in the way of extra space and our friend Gareth has a spare room, but he's probably not the best candidate."

Bray rolled his eyes, Roose snorted, Jackson fumed, and Eleanor leaned back into the far corner of the couch keeping Foster close to her. Mac chuckled. Or it might have been a cough. Eleanor couldn't tell.

Of everyone present in the room, Vixen was the calmest, as though she spent her life dealing with one crisis after another and this one ranked low on her panic meter. Eleanor envied her.

"Mommy, you're holding me too tight." Foster announced to the room and bounced on her lap.

"Mommy?" Jackson, Bray, and Vixen asked at the same time.

"Like I said. You all can wait. I think there are other things we should talk about first." Mac looked down at Foster. "Want to take a walk? Get some of that energy out of you? We can head over to Bray and Vixen's place, since that's where you'll be staying."

"They are?" Once more Jackson, Bray, and Vixen spoke at the same time.

"We are?" Eleanor chorused a few seconds behind them.

For the second time in her life, a shifter took over Eleanor's life. At least she assumed Mac and the others were shifters. Why else would Wayne send her to them?

VIXEN'S SHIFT
A SILVER SENTINEL SHORT STORY

VIXEN bounced on the balls of her feet in a small clearing far away from the prying eyes of the rest of the pack, and Bray did his best not to stare at the way her breasts moved with her. After thirty seconds of staring at the tree trunk behind Vixen's left shoulder, Bray's will surrendered to the part of him who still giggled when of the boys in the pack spelled the word "boobies" on the calculator (5318008, then turned upside down), and openly admired the curves and swells of her breasts and the nipples hardened, not from arousal, but the chill in the evening air. Although, if Vixen didn't hurry and shift, Bray was close to changing that.

"You've done it before." Bray's patience ran thin, not because of Vixen, but because of the beast who lived inside her. The griffin was fucking scary, no matter if Bray was her mate. While both Vixen and her griffin had the same calculating eyes, Vixen's at least showed a hint of warmth when she looked at Bray or the boys in the pack.

"Yeah, and she ripped out a man's spine."

"Well, she also disemboweled him, too." The griffin's killing instinct was awesome to witness.

"You aren't helping."

"And you're stalling." Bray grinned at his mate. In front of the rest of the pack, she was confident and secure, but in front of him, and only him, she'd allowed him to see the hints of vulnerability. His heart raced when she revealed those glimpses of the female she kept hidden away from everyone else.

"I'm having two conversations right now, one with you and one with *her*." Vixen rolled her eyes at the mention of her griffin. She still didn't trust the beast and probably wouldn't for quite some time. "For what it's worth, she's on the same side as you."

"And you're still stalling." He stepped closer. Bray's need to have Vixen right there in the middle of the woods was winning its battle against his self-control.

"But what if she attacks you?"

"She won't." They'd had the same argument for a month. "I promise."

Bray wanted Vixen to shift. It wasn't healthy to keep an animal locked up inside, especially one as powerful as a griffin. The same way, it wasn't safe to allow the animal free rein for long periods of time. Shifters needed to maintain a healthy balance with their animals or they risked turning feral and eventually being hunted by their own kind before the animal attacked a human.

Vixen, on the other hand, would be perfectly content keeping her griffin locked away indefinitely.

"You don't know that."

"I do." He didn't, but he wasn't going to admit as much to Vixen. What Bray *did* have was faith that her griffin would recognize him as her mate and not attempt to use any of the sharper parts of her body against him. Plus, his wolf was more than capable of standing up to her griffin. He'd done it before when the beast first appeared and was completely out of control with revenge on the mind.

Vixen crossed her arms over her chest, covering her distracting breasts. "Don't. Lie. I can tell when you're lying."

"Vi, just shift already. I swear, nothing bad is going to happen. But if you keep putting it off the peanut gallery is going to get impatient and figure out where we are, come out here, and then we will have something to worry about."

Both Vixen and Bray agreed shifting outside and away from the rest of the pack was probably for the best. Unfortunately, the pack wasn't known for following directions on the best of days, and the chance of seeing Vixen's griffin again made for a truly horrible day for following directions.

Vixen stomped her foot and dropped her arms. "Fine."

Bray struggled not to laugh. If he'd learned anything in the past month as her mate, Vixen did not enjoy it one bit when Bray found her cute. Or adorable. Especially adorable. The last time he called her adorable, she had growled at him in this cute non-wolf way so of course Bray laughed. And, of course, Vixen elbowed him in the ribs. It still hurt to take a deep breath three weeks later.

"As soon as you shift and your griffin settles, I'll shift and then our animals can play."

"Don't say I didn't warn you." Vixen had run out of excuses. Her griffin had probably achieved a level of impatience Vixen couldn't keep in check.

"Duly noted."

The oddity of Vixen's shift wasn't how the griffin finally appeared. Like all other shifters, the change just happened. One minute a human shaped female stood in front of Bray and the next, a griffin. Granted, the griffin exceeded the magnificence of most other shifters, so the mundane nature of the shift was easily ignored.

Of course, the ordinary nature of the shifting would have probably gone ignored even if Vixen didn't have a griffin inside of her because Vixen's animal talked. The griffin actually spoke, and not in the silly way some dogs on the YouTube talked, but genuine words and somewhat complete sentences.

"Finally." The griffin hissed at Bray from across the suddenly impossibly small clearing.

Bray brushed his neatly trimmed nails against the whiskers on his cheek. He had no idea how to refer to the griffin. Vixen and her beast had a unique relationship in that they were separate, but during the first nearly forty years of Vixen's life, the griffin lived inside Vixen's mind and influenced her actions.

The griffin cocked her head to the side and peered at Bray. Except instead of the bright yellow iris completely covering her eye, the whites of Vixen's eyes showed through.

Good. The griffin was allowing Vixen to stay close instead of shuttering her inside and keeping his mate completely in the dark.

In a blink of an eye, the raptor's eyes returned. "Wolf?"

Bray's eyebrows shot up. He fully planned on enticing the griffin into a conversation, but the legend appeared to be as curious as he was. "Later. A few questions first."

"Now." And impatient.

"Later." Bray couldn't stop himself from grinning. The griffin was like a toddler. A toddler with razors for fingers, but a toddler nonetheless. The rest of the boys were going to be in for a treat if they ever trusted the griffin to run with the entire pack. "We'll hunt later, I promise."

"Sssay that a lot." The sibilant esses emphasized her hiss. The griffin's eyes narrowed, and she jutted her head forward, closer to Bray.

He did. "But only when I mean it."

The griffin sat back on her left hip, letting her right leg splay out slightly with her left leg tucked under her body. She resembled a pup or cub sitting like that, cute and almost cuddly. "Fine."

Bray cringed inside, but didn't allow the griffin to see it. Whenever Vixen said the word fine, it never boded well for him. He imagined it was no different with her griffin. "Mac found an old journal of his ancestors, one that spoke about Great Shifters. Is that what you are?"

The griffin's head cocked to the side as she considered the question. "Don't know."

Not that he expected her to know, but it was worth asking.

"Alwaysss here."

"What? No, I came here when I was younger."

"No." The griffin stomped her front foot. "Alwaysss here. Waiting."

Apparently talking with the griffin was going to be like solving one of those logic problems where the answer only made sense to the creator. "You? Waiting inside Vixen?"

"Yesss." The griffin hissed, clearly happy with Bray's understanding.

"We'll leave the where from to Mac. How about that?"

"Good." The griffin's head bobbed up and down.

If Bray didn't think the griffin would take as much offense as Vixen, he would have told her just how adorable she was. Except the whole point of this shifting exercise was to convince the griffin to agree to some terms. Terms that would make Vixen more comfortable with her animal and would also likely give the pack a better chance of survival. He didn't put it past any of the boys to offend the griffin and find themselves without a spine. And as far as Bray knew, shifters couldn't just regrow a spine that had been ripped out by a petulant griffin.

"Do you want to come out more?"

"Yesss." Her eyes narrowed, as though she knew there would be a catch. Clever griffin.

"Remember what happened the last time you came out?"

The griffin's beak gaped open what Bray figured was a grin. "Yesss. Bad men."

"Yes, bad men, and you protected the pack. Thank you. But you can't do that all the time. In fact, if you want to come out again, Vixen wants you to promise that you'll behave and listen to her."

"I lisssten." While technically true, she did indeed listen to Vixen, she also ignored Vixen when it didn't fit with her wants.

"But you have to live together, right? So, you can't just listen and do what you want. You have to agree to follow her directions sometimes."

"Why?"

Why? Well, wasn't that the million-dollar question? Bray racked his brain in an attempt to come up with a reasonable answer the griffin would accept. "She listens to you when you're inside."

"No more."

Well, shit. He'd need to talk to Vi about that. The griffin had kept her alive for nearly forty years. Ignoring the griffin now might actually be dangerous. But that was another argument for another day. "She won't let you come out again if you don't take her advice."

"Fine."

"Fine?"

"Fine."

Bray came to realize they'd just repeat the word back and forth. The griffin really was like a toddler sometimes.

"You'll listen to her like she used to listen to you?"

"Yesss." The griffin's talon tapped against the dirt. "Ssshe lissstensss to me?"

"Yes, she'll listen to you again."

The griffin grinned. "Ssshe yellsss."

Bray shrugged, "that sounds like Vi."

"Wolf?"

"Soon." It was all too easy. Bray expected the griffin to argue more, but instead she agreed without too much of a fight. "And you have to promise not to hurt the boys in the pack."

"Never. Vixen lovesss pack. Never hurt pack. Never hurt you."

"I know, but Vi needed to know it, too."

"Wolf?"

Bray laughed. He couldn't help himself. The griffin probably would have agreed to a lifetime as a vegetarian if she got to see his wolf. "Okay, okay. Wolf. But wolf can't talk."

"I fix."

"You fix? How?"

"Wolf."

"Okay, wolf." Somehow Bray knew that was the closest answer he'd get from her. Whatever the reason, the griffin was obsessed with Bray's wolf. Bray made quick work of stripping off his clothes and piled them next to Vixen's. They'd come back to the clearing to shift back and dress before returning to the Lodge, but for the time being the clothes would be safe.

"Back." The griffin growled out.

Bray stepped away from her. "What?"

"Her. Not you."

"Her?"

"Vixen. Close. Not quiet."

"Really?"

The griffin might have rolled her eyes, but she definitely let out a tiny huff. "Likesss watching."

Bray chuckled. Not only would he have to contend with Vixen having conversations with her griffin aloud, but they'd also have to deal with the griffin talking to Vixen. Although, in the scheme of things, a griffin talking to herself fell far down the list of weird things Bray never thought he'd have to worry about.

"Are you ready?"

"Yesss. Wolf." The griffin bounced up and down on her front legs in anticipation of Bray's wolf finally making an appearance.

Bray winked at the griffin before he let his wolf come forward.

Wolf!

The griffin's voice appeared in the wolf's mind. It was as though the griffin had been speaking aloud, but inside a cone of silence and only the wolf and Bray could hear.

You try!

The wolf scrambled backwards while looking for help from Bray. Not that Bray had any knowledge of how to send thoughts into the mind of someone else, but the Wolf didn't know that.

Think.

Bray wondered if the griffin meant the wolf or him.

Both. Yes.

What? Wait. Bray hadn't thought about sending his thoughts the griffin's way. Did that mean the griffin could read both the man's and beast's thoughts?

Yes. I tell you I fix. Now wolf try.

Oh God, this would be interesting. His wolf cared about two things. Food and his mate. Occasionally, he considered the well-being of the pack, but unless Vi was directly involved, he didn't seem to care.

Vixen's laughter danced through Bray's mind and he heard her as clearly as if she had been standing next to him and not hiding inside her griffin.

Well, that was unexpected.

I might be willing to concede that there are some benefits that come with having a griffin locked inside of you. Vixen's husky voice wrapped itself around Bray's mind, and he shuddered. It was better than when she purred in his ear.

Wolf try now. Yes?

Sure, why not.

Hunt now?

At least the wolf hadn't brought up fucking.

Later. Hunt now.

Bray banged his head against the invisible wall inside his imagination. *Can we hide?*

I haven't yet found a way, but I'm sure my feathered alter-ego can help us with that particular need.

Play with wolf?

Yes, you can play with Bray's wolf.

Good.

As quickly as the griffin had invaded his mind, she left. Bray presumed she had also left Vixen alone, but wouldn't know until they shifted back. He trusted his wolf wouldn't let the griffin get into too much trouble. So, for the time being, he settled back, napped, and let his wolf play with the griffin.

ACKNOWLEDGMENTS

Sitting down to write an acknowledgment page is much like making an acceptance speech at an award's show. It's more than likely that you will forget someone and then have to spend hours on the phone apologizing for the misstep. And God help you, if it's your mother. So, I should probably get that one out of the way first, right? I need to acknowledge my parents, especially my mother, who have supported me and define the phrase unconditional love.

The readers of the Broken Peak Pack and the Sentinels of the Silver Orb. Without them, there would be no Vixen and Bray.

Love and thanks to Cassandra V. She's my cheerleader, friend, and taskmaster.

I would be remiss in not thanking my friends and family, who put up with me during my seclusion in the writing cave and constantly offer their support and love.

Finally, and of course not least, the wonderful individuals who are responsible for the creation of the collector's edition of the Broken Peak Pack Omnibus: Kasey S., Sherry M., Meg M., Pyndan, Erin C., Rhel, Kieran, Rafael P, Sarah, and Melanie B. Little did they know that by supporting one little Kickstarter, they'd find a permanent spot on my acknowledgments page.

ABOUT THE AUTHOR

Jules Crisare loves writing sexy shifter romances. The growly and dominant males of Broken Peak and the Silver Sentinels are the ones bending to the strong wills of the smart heroines who cross their paths. Seriously, only strong heroines need apply to capture the hearts of these sexy alphas. Get your shifter loving fingers ready to turn those pages and explore the world of the Sentinels of the Silver Orb.

www.JCrisare.com

www.ingramcontent.com/pod-product-compliance
Lightning Source LLC
Chambersburg PA
CBHW031249210726
48287CB00003B/963